D0398947

Chocolate Chips and Trumpet Tricks

Nancy Simpson Levene

Chariot Books™
David C. Cook Publishing Co.

Chariot Books™ is an imprint of David C. Cook Publishing Co.
David C. Cook Publishing Co., Elgin, Illinois 60120
David C. Cook Publishing Co., Weston, Ontario
Nova Distribution Ltd., Newton Abbot, England

CHOCOLATE CHIPS AND TRUMPET TRICKS
© 1994 by Nancy R. Simpson

Unless otherwise noted, Scripture quotations are from *The Living Bible*,
© 1971, Tyndale House Publishers, Wheaton, IL 60187. Used by permission.

Scripture marked (NASB) are taken from *New American Standard Bible*, © the
Lockman Foundation 1960, 1962, 1963, 1968, 1971, 1972, 1973, 1975, 1977.

Designed by Bill Paetzold
Cover illustration by Neal Hughes
Internal illustrations by Ann Iosa
First Printing, 1994
Printed in the United States of America
98 97 96 95 94 5 4 3 2 1
Library of Congress Cataloging-in-Publication Data
Levene, Nancy S., 1949-
Chocolate chips, trumpet tricks, and other devotions with Alex / by Nancy
Simpson Levene.
p.   cm.
Summary: Stories featuring the high-spirited Alex, her family and friends,
demonstrate what it means to be a good Christian. Questions follow each story.
ISBN 0-7814-0103-8
[1. Christian life—Fiction. 2. Conduct of life—Fiction. 3. Family life—Fiction.] I.
Title.
PZ7.L5724Ci   1949
[Fic]—dc20   93-36195
CIP   AC

Contents

To Jesus
who feeds us daily
from His abundant storehouse,
and
To Nancy Hutchings
whose love and compassion
nourish a wealth of friends.

ACKNOWLEDGMENTS

I thank my daughter, Cara, for her support and creativity, and especially for contributing the story lines for "Birthday Blues," "The Secret Password," and "The Truth and Nothing But . . . ."

I thank my editor, Sue Reck, for her patience and hard work, particularly in shortening and lengthening these chapters many times over.

And I thank God for suggesting all these stories to my mind and helping me to fit them all together.

Introduction

Have you ever tried to go a whole day without eating? How about a whole week? That would not be easy or good for you. Without food, we feel weak, tired, and sick. We need food to stay alive, and we need the right kinds of food to be healthy and active. Unfortunately, we can't be very healthy if we only drink chocolate milk shakes!

Just as our bodies need the right kinds of food every day, so do our minds and spirits. What kind of food do you think God put on the earth especially for our minds and spirits? Did you guess it? It's the Bible!

The Bible feeds our minds and spirits with the very thoughts of God. It shows us how to think the right way and how to make the right decisions in life. Once you begin to read the Bible regularly, marvelous things happen in your life. But don't just take it from me. Take it from Alex! Turn the page and see how God and His Word guide Alex through her real-life adventures!

May God bless you as you eat and drink from the table of the King.

Nancy Simpson Levene

Chocolate Chip
Surprise

Love your neighbor as yourself!
Matthew 19:19b

JANIE, look out!" Alex cried. She slid
across the kitchen floor and dove
underneath Janie just as the opened bag
of chocolate chips fell off the counter. It
landed KERPLOP! in Alex's lap, spilling
its contents all over Alex's legs. Not a
single chip, however, hit the floor.

"Janie, you gotta be more careful," Alex
told her best friend. At that moment,
Alex's mother entered the kitchen.

"Alex, I need to pick up your brother,
Rudy, from his music lessons. I'll be gone

about half an hour. You girls will be all right here alone for that long, won't you?"

"Oh, sure," all four girls replied at once.

Mother didn't even seem to notice Alex sitting on the floor, and she hurried out the front door.

Mother had not been gone five minutes when the doorbell suddenly rang.

"Peek out the front window and see who it is," Alex told Lorraine.

Lorraine left the kitchen and returned almost immediately.

"It's Gretchen," Lorraine whispered to Alex. "Do you want me to let her in?"

"No," Janie replied quickly. "Gretchen is a bossy know-it-all!"

"Shhh!" Lorraine whispered. "She'll hear you. We don't want you to let her in."

"But that will really hurt her feelings," Alex protested.

"Just don't answer the door, and she'll think nobody's home," Julie said.

The doorbell rang and rang. The girls stayed absolutely still, making no noise.

Soon, a loud banging replaced the

rings of the doorbell.

"I know you're in there, Alex!" Gretchen shouted. "Please let me in."

Alex frowned and moved for the door. "We really ought to let her in," she said.

"No," all three of her friends responded. "Gretchen would spoil everything!"

Alex stood where she was and listened as Gretchen rang the bell a few more times. Then, finally, the noise stopped. Slowly, Alex and the other girls stepped over to the front window and peeked outside. They watched Gretchen walk across the street and disappear inside her own house. The girls stared at one another with guilty faces. Gretchen had been crying and walked with her head down and shoulders slumped.

The girls returned to their cookie baking, but somehow their good time was spoiled. Even smelling the delicious aroma of warm chocolate chips did not help them feel any better.

"I guess we should have let Gretchen

come inside," Janie finally admitted.

"Maybe we could go over to her house and apologize," Julie suggested.

"We could invite her over for some cookies," Lorraine offered.

"That's a great idea!" Alex exclaimed. "First, let's make her a card with lots of pictures and things. We can write 'We're Sorry' on it, and leave it inside her front door. Then we can ring the doorbell and hide. As soon as she opens it, we can jump out and say, 'Surprise!' "

Alex's friends liked that idea. They sat down to work right away. In no time, they had made a colorful card for Gretchen.

The girls left the house by the back door and sneaked through several backyards before crossing the street. Darting behind parked cars and bushes, they made their way back to Gretchen's house. Alex carefully opened the outer storm door and placed the card between it and the front door. She then rang the doorbell and darted behind a row of bushes where her friends were hiding. The girls covered their mouths with their hands to keep their giggles from escaping.

Gretchen opened the door. Alex and the others watched her read the card

and give a loud gasp. Then all four girls popped out of the bushes.

"SURPRISE!" they hollered at the top of their lungs.

"Ahhhhh!" Gretchen screamed in fright. Then she began to laugh. So did the others. Soon, arm in arm, the five girls skipped back across the street to Alex's house.

Mother pulled up with Rudy just as

the girls reached the front steps.

"Alex, what are you doing?" Mother wanted to know.

"Oh, we just invited Gretchen to eat cookies with us," Alex told her mother.

"Oh, that's nice," replied Mother.

Yes, it is nice, thought Alex as she followed her friends inside the house. *It is nice that we are all friends!*

Amen.

 ## Food for Thought

Why do you think the girls pretended they were not home when Gretchen rang the doorbell? If you were Gretchen, how would you feel? Why was it important for the girls to apologize to Gretchen?

In this story, the food from the Bible is:

Love others as yourself.

Trumpet Tricks

Work hard and become a leader;
be lazy and never succeed.
Proverbs 12:24

HEY, everybody, we have a substitute teacher in band. Quick, let's switch instruments!" cried Eddie Thompson.

"Brussels sprouts!" Alex exclaimed when she heard the news. "Quick, Lorraine, I'll trade you my trumpet for your baritone."

"Okay," Lorraine agreed. The two girls quickly swapped instruments. It was always so much fun when their regular band instructor, Mr. Sharp, was absent and a substitute teacher was called. The children would then switch instruments. Of course, no one could play the swapped instruments very well. Then when the substitute teacher would ask them to play their music, a most horrendous sound would emerge.

Upon arriving in the band room, Alex saw that the substitute teacher was a nice-looking young woman. She had never been to their school before. Alex almost felt sorry about switching instruments. It was more fun to pull the trick on someone older and grumpier.

"Hello, my name is Miss Paris," said the young woman after everyone had taken their seats. "I am your substitute teacher."

Miss Paris passed out the sheet music and then held up her hands, signaling everyone to get ready to play. Alex tensed. This was the note they'd all been waiting for—the first terrible, awful note!

Miss Paris lowered her hands in the conductor's fashion.

BLAAAAAAAHHHHEEEEE! The

instruments groaned, wailed, and screeched. Miss Paris had such a shocked look on her face that Alex could hardly keep from laughing. She blew her hardest on Lorraine's baritone.

Finally, the music ended. Everyone gasped for air. Miss Paris held a hand to her head as if it hurt. She tried to smile.

"Well," Miss Paris said after a moment's hesitation, "I can see that the music is coming along. Uh, why don't we try something else?"

Band class went on, and the children played several more pieces. Finally, with a sigh of relief, Miss Paris collected all the sheet music, and the students got ready to leave.

"Oh, there's one thing I almost forgot to tell you," Miss Paris announced. "If any of you trumpet players would like to play a solo for the upcoming concert, sign your name on the sheet of paper here on the desk. Tryouts are a week from Friday."

Lorraine looked at Alex. Alex nodded her head yes and motioned for Lorraine to go sign Alex's name on the sign-up sheet.

"Thank you, Alex," Miss Paris said to Lorraine as she read the name on the sheet. The class laughed.

Alex practiced her solo piece after dinner every night. She even got up half an hour earlier in the mornings for further practice.

Alex worked hard and began to feel confident with the music. By the early part of the second week, she had it memorized and could play the whole song easily without looking at the music.

"Sounds like you're gonna get that

solo," Janie encouraged Alex, after listening to Alex practice one afternoon after school. "It sounds really great!"

However, the next day in band class, Nicholas Freese had a different idea. "You might as well forget it," he told Alex. "I'm going to get the trumpet solo."

"Have you been practicing for it?" Alex asked nervously.

"I don't need to practice," retorted Nicholas, his nose in the air. "I'm better than you without practicing."

"Brussels sprouts," Alex muttered. She felt like socking Nicholas in the nose. But instead, she went home and practiced even harder. And every night, she asked God to help her do her best in the tryouts.

Finally, the big day arrived.

"Don't worry about Nicholas," Janie told Alex as they waited for the tryouts to begin. "Just go up on that stage and play your best."

Alex took a deep breath and climbed the stairs to the stage. She, Nicholas, and two other trumpet players were trying out for the solo.

Mr. Sharp had them line up in the order he wanted them to play. To Alex's dismay, she was first.

"Please help me, Lord Jesus," Alex prayed quickly as she raised her trumpet to her lips. She blew the first note loud and strong. From then on, it was easy. The notes flowed out of the trumpet in perfect form. It almost seemed as if the instrument had memorized the piece and was playing the music itself.

When she finished, Alex looked at Mr. Sharp. The band director stared at her, his mouth wide open in surprise.

"I have never heard any student play that piece so well," he told her.

Alex smiled. Janie held up her hands in a victory sign.

Next, a boy played the solo, then another girl. Neither of them got through the piece without several mistakes.

Finally, it was Nicholas's turn. He did not look so confident now. Raising his trumpet to his lips, he played the piece through, stumbling here and there. His trumpet playing sounded flat compared to Alex's. It was obvious to everyone in the room who should get the solo.

"I thank all of you for trying out," Mr. Sharp told the students. He smiled at Alex. "You got the solo."

"YIPPEE!" Janie cried. Alex could only grin. She had found out firsthand what prayer and hard work could do.

"Thank You, Lord," she whispered.

Amen.

 Food for Thought

In this story, how did hard work pay off for Alex? What about prayer? What was the result of Nicholas's laziness? How did the Lord come through for Alex?

In this story, the food from the Bible is:

_____

Hard work pays off.

18

Duet Disaster

The greatest love is shown when a person lays
down his life for his friends.
John 15:13

WE are going to sing with the adult
choir at the Christmas pageant," Mrs.
Piper told the children's choir. "We need
several children to sing short solos and
two children to sing a longer duet. If you
would like to sing any of these parts,
please let me know tonight."

Alex sat up straight in her chair and
listened intently as Mrs. Piper talked
about the duet part. She smiled. She
would love to do the duet and knew just
the person she wanted for a partner. She

glanced over at Sarah Cooke. Sarah was a year older than Alex and had a terrific voice. Alex was a good singer too. She knew they would be dynamite together!

"Oh, Alex, let's try out for the duet part!" exclaimed Alex's best friend, Janie. "Wouldn't that be so neat to sing a duet in the Christmas pageant?"

"Well, maybe," Alex hesitated. How could she tell Janie that she didn't want to sing with her?

"Aw, come on, Alex," Janie nudged her best friend. "It would be fun!"

"Let me think about it," Alex replied.

At break time, while Janie was getting a drink of water, Alex walked over to Sarah and sat down beside her.

"Are you going to try out for the Christmas duet Mrs. Piper was talking about?" Alex asked Sarah.

"I would, but I don't have a partner," Sarah replied.

"Would you want to be partners with me?" Alex asked hopefully.

"Sure!" Sarah agreed immediately.

"Let's go tell Mrs. Piper right away."

The two girls found Mrs. Piper out in the hallway, talking to a group of children.

"Why, that's splendid!" the choir director exclaimed when Alex and Sarah told her they would like to sing the duet. "You girls don't need to try out. I already know you would be perfect for the duet!"

Alex skipped back to the choir room with Sarah. She felt very happy, until she noticed that Janie had returned to the room and was waiting for her.

Janie could not ask Alex any questions, however, as Mrs. Piper clapped her hands for attention. Before starting the choir on a song, she made an announcement.

"We have two people to sing our duet—Alex Brackenbury and Sarah Cooke. You girls will need to pick up your music before you leave tonight."

Alex nodded at Mrs. Piper. She then cringed in her seat and waited for the outburst from Janie. She knew whatever was coming would be bad.

"Alex!" Janie exploded beside her. "Is

what Mrs. Piper said true? Are you going to sing the duet with Sarah Cooke?"

"Now, now, Janie," Alex turned to face her best friend. "Take it easy. I'm sorry. It all just sort of happened at break time. I mean, I didn't want to hurt your feelings or anything but . . ."

Alex gave up. Janie had left her seat beside Alex and moved to an empty chair at the back of the room. She did not speak to Alex for the rest of the evening.

The next morning, Janie did not walk to school with Alex. She did not play with her at recess, or sit with her at lunch. Most of their friends sided with Janie.

"You shouldn't have been so mean to Janie," they told Alex.

"I can't believe you did that to Janie, Alex."

"You should have been honest and told her you didn't want to sing with her."

Alex, in turn, began to spend more time with Sarah. They met quite often after school to practice their duet.

Although Alex tried to tell herself that she could get along fine without Janie, deep down inside she knew better. She missed her best friend

terribly. No one could ever really take Janie's place.

Finally, one lonely miserable day, Alex knocked on Janie's front door.

"What are you doing here?" Janie snarled as soon as she opened the door.

"I, uh, was wondering if we could ever be friends again," Alex stammered.

"Hmmmmpf!" Janie folded her arms across her chest. "You're the one who messed up our friendship in the first place. You went behind my back and asked Sarah to sing with you. You could have been honest and told me you wanted to sing with her."

Alex stared at her former best friend. What Janie had said was true. She was guilty.

"Janie, you're right," Alex admitted. "I did things the wrong way and I'm really sorry. Is there any way you can forgive me? I'll do anything!"

Janie frowned at Alex. "Anything?" she asked. "Then go tell Mrs. Piper you don't want to sing the duet with Sarah. If you do that, we can be friends again." With that, Janie slammed the door shut in Alex's face.

Alex stared at the door for a moment. She could hardly believe her ears. Had Janie really said she must give up the duet to be her friend again?

All afternoon, Alex thought seriously about Janie's demand. What was the right thing to do? Finally, she decided to ask the one person who would know.

"Dear Lord Jesus," Alex prayed, "please show me what to do."

As she thought further about it, Alex asked herself which was more important—singing a duet or keeping a friend? The more she thought about it, the more Alex realized that a friend was more important than all the duets in the world. As she got ready for choir practice that evening, Alex knew what she must do.

As soon as she arrived at the church, Alex told Mrs. Piper and Sarah that she could not sing the duet. She explained the situation with Janie as best she could. Although the choir director and Sarah were disappointed, they seemed to understand.

Before the singing began, Mrs. Piper announced to the choir, "Alex has decided that she cannot sing the Christmas duet with Sarah. If there is anyone who would like to take her place, please see me at break time."

Alex shrunk down in her seat. She hoped she was doing the right thing. She knew she had just let down Mrs. Piper and Sarah. Alex glanced over at Janie. Her former best friend had a shocked look on her face.

At break time, Janie ran over to Alex. There were tears in Janie's eyes.

"You mean you really gave up the duet for me?" Janie asked in a choked voice.

Alex felt tears sting her eyes too. She shrugged. "Sure, you're my best friend."

"Oh, Alex!" Janie grabbed her friend in a big hug. As Alex hugged her back, she smiled. She knew now that she had done the right thing.

"Thank You, Lord," she prayed. "Thanks for giving me back my best friend."

Amen.

Food for Thought

Was Alex wrong not to tell Janie the truth about wanting to sing the duet with Sarah? What did Alex sacrifice to mend her friendship with Janie? What did Jesus sacrifice for us? When you sacrifice something for your friends, you are being like Jesus.

In this story, the food from the Bible is:

Sacrifice for your friends.

Double Chocolate Bonus

For if you give, you will get! Your gift will return to you in full and overflowing measure, pressed down, shaken together to make room for more, and running over.
Luke 6:38a, b

COME ON, Alex. Can't we get rid of these kids and go off on our own?" Janie pleaded.

"No, I'm sorry, Janie," Alex replied. "I promised Mom I'd take Rudy and his friend Jason to the school carnival."

"But why did you promise that?" Janie complained. "You know how much we enjoy going together to the carnival."

"I know, and we've gone together every year for the last three years," Alex told her best friend. "This is Rudy and Jason's first year to go to the carnival. Besides, there was no one else to take them. Jason's mom is busy at the church, and my mom has to get ready for a party she's having tonight."

"Oh, Alex," Janie sighed.

"Aw, come on, Janie. You'll see. It'll be even more fun than going by ourselves," promised Alex.

"Oh, sure," Janie scowled. She watched unhappily as Alex bought a supply of tickets for each boy.

"Here are ten tickets for each of you," Alex handed Rudy and Jason their tickets.

"Only ten tickets?" Rudy asked. "Can't we do more than ten things?"

"Well, we'll see," answered Alex. "Hey look!" she pointed to a nearby booth. "There's the Hoop Shot."

"Awesome!" Rudy exclaimed. "Come on, Jason. Let's go!"

"Okay, boys," said Alex, catching up to them, "you gotta throw the ball through the hoop to get a prize."

"I know, I know!" Rudy cried. Before

Alex could stop him, he grabbed a ball and threw it way over the hoop. It bounced over the back of the booth and into another carnival stand. The man in charge had to run after the ball.

"Rudy, don't be in such a hurry," Alex told her brother. "You gotta stand on this line, see? Then you carefully aim for the hoop . . . like this." Alex demonstrated for Rudy and Jason. She scored an easy basket.

"Very good," said the man in charge. "You just won a prize!"

"Oh, I was just showing them how to play," Alex smiled.

"Are you two girls the baby-sitters?" the man asked Alex and Janie.

"Yeah, we're taking the boys around the carnival," Alex answered.

"Well, that's a wonderful thing for you to do," the man said. "Let me give a prize to each of you girls."

"Gee, thanks!" Alex and Janie cried as the man handed each of them a pair of neon green sunglasses.

The boys each tried the hoop toss. Rudy won a toy airplane for dunking two balls in the net, and Jason got a rubber ball as a booby prize for failing to make a basket.

"It's okay, Jason," Alex comforted the younger boy. "You just have to learn to stand still and concentrate on the net. Don't worry, you'll get it next time."

The boys moved on to the next booth. There, two wooden bottles stood close together on a stool, with a third bottle stacked on top of them.

"Aha!" Alex exclaimed. "The old Bottle Throw! This is my favorite booth. Watch this, boys, and I'll show you my expert moves!"

"Oh, brother," Janie sighed.

Alex grinned at Janie and moved up to the rail in front of the booth. She gave the lady at the booth a ticket. The lady handed her three balls.

Alex grabbed one of the balls. She leaned back and began an exaggerated pitcher's windup. But before she could complete it, Rudy called out loudly to one of his friends who stood on the other side of the room.

"Hey, Jeremy, here's my sister! You know, the pitcher, the one I was telling you about? Come on over and watch her smash this stack of bottles!"

At the sound of Rudy's voice, everybody in the immediate area turned and fixed their eyes on Alex.

"Shhhh!" Alex hissed at Rudy, feeling very embarrassed by all the attention.

Jeremy and his friends ran over to Rudy. They gathered around Alex, crossed their arms over their chests, and stared at her, waiting for a pitching miracle.

Alex sighed. Once again, she leaned back into a pitching stance and began her windup. The lady working the booth stepped behind a large pillar for protection.

Janie giggled. Alex ignored her. With determination written all over her face, Alex drew back her arm and let go of the

ball with a powerful throw. WHAM!
BLAM! The ball struck the exact center
where the three bottles met, sending all
three flying through the air. One hit the
pillar where the lady was hiding.

"Wow!" a little boy breathed.

"Sign her up for the Royals!" several
people cried as they applauded Alex's
throw.

Everyone laughed.

"I still have two throws left," Alex
told the lady behind the booth.

"No, please," the lady replied, looking
carefully at the bottles to see if they
were damaged. "I will give you a prize

for your one throw."

Alex smiled. "Okay," she agreed. The lady handed her a large plastic flute.

"Neato!" the boys all cried. They gathered around Alex in admiration.

After that event, Alex and Janie were continually surrounded by small boys. They followed them from booth to booth. Alex and Janie looked like two Pied Pipers with a town full of children skipping after them.

The boys shared their prizes freely with Alex and Janie. Some even decided to win prizes especially for the two girls.

"This is for you," one little boy shyly handed Janie a purple and white bracelet he had won at the fishing pond.

"Why, thank you," Janie smiled. She added the bracelet to a sack full of similar treasures. "Gee, Alex," Janie said happily, "I think we're getting much more than we ever could have gotten by ourselves!"

"I know," Alex grinned. "Isn't this fun?"

"Yeah, it is," Janie admitted.

Just then, a small boy ran up to Alex and Janie. He was carrying a large chocolate cake. "Guess what?" he cried. "I won this cake at the Cakewalk. Come on, let's eat it!"

Everybody laughed. Alex and Janie sat down on the floor, surrounded by a group of little children. They munched and munched on the chocolate cake until it was gone.

"You know, Alex, I think you are right," Janie said, licking her fingers. "This is much more fun than being off by ourselves. I feel like I've done something good by taking these kids around the carnival, and I've also had a great time myself!"

"Right," Alex agreed. "I've found that when you do something good for others, you always get something back in return. It's kind of like you get a double bonus."

"Hey, Alex, look what I just won!" Rudy suddenly cried, running up to his big sister. In his arms was another chocolate cake!

"Oh, no," Alex chuckled.

"Well, I think you got a double *chocolate* bonus, Alex!" Janie exclaimed. They laughed and laughed.

Amen.

 Food for Thought

What did Alex and Janie give to Rudy and his friends? What did Janie learn about giving to other people? What did Alex mean by a double bonus?

In this story, the food from the Bible is:

When you give, you will get.

Pieces, Parts, and Problems

Patience develops strength of character in us
and helps us trust God more each time we
use it until finally our hope and faith are
strong and steady.
Romans 5:4

ALEX made a giant leap to stand right
in front of her father. "The parts for my
bicycle were delivered today. Can we fix
it tonight? I'll help you."

"Oh, Firecracker, I'm sorry," Father
said, using his nickname for Alex. "I
have some very important paper work to
do tonight. The bicycle will have to wait
until tomorrow night."

"But everybody's gonna ride their
bikes to school tomorrow," Alex
complained. "I'll be the only one in the

neighborhood without a bike."

"I'm sorry, Firecracker," Father replied, "but I have to work tonight. You'll have to be patient and wait."

"There's that word again! Patient! I hate that word," Alex complained to herself. "I don't want to be patient."

Alex went outside to the garage and stared at her broken ten-speed bicycle. There, lying beside it, was the package containing the parts to fix it.

As Alex stared at the package, a sudden thought came to her. Why couldn't she fix her bicycle? She'd watched Father fix lots of things before. All he ever did was read the directions and follow them. She could do that!

Ripping open the package, Alex found several metal pieces, a plastic bag containing bolts, screws, and nuts, and another bag containing various colored wires. Alex opened both bags and laid everything out carefully, just as she had seen Father do many times.

Opening the instruction booklet, Alex

read through the first few instructions. They were a little confusing, but Alex was sure she would figure it out as she went. She hammered and shoved and twisted and bent one part after another,

until she completed Step A. With a satisfied sigh, Alex set the twisted and dented metal parts down beside her.

Just then, Alex's large black labrador came running into the garage. He made a giant sweep with his tail, and scattered the parts for Alex's bicycle across the floor.

"T-Bone!" Alex hollered. "Get out of here!" She turned the giant dog around and led him out of the garage.

Then, to Alex's dismay, a car suddenly pulled into the driveway. It did not stop, but continued on into the open garage.

"Wait! Stop!" she cried in horror, but it was no use. Alex's teenaged sister, Barbara, was driving. Loud music blared out the car windows.

The car rolled into the garage right over all the piles of metal parts and gadgets. POP! CRACK! CRUNCH! The metal pieces broke under the tires. Then an extra loud BLAM! sounded, and Alex saw firsthand what a sharp piece of metal can do to a tire.

Barbara jerked the car to a stop. She opened the car door and leaned out. "Did something happen?" she asked Alex.

Before Alex could answer, the door from the kitchen to the garage suddenly opened. Father stood in the doorway.

"What's going on out here?" he cried. He ran down the steps and into the garage. He stared openmouthed at the flat tire. Then his gaze fell on the crushed pieces of metal littering the garage floor.

"Will somebody please tell me what is going on?" he asked again.

"Don't look at me," Barbara replied. "I just drove the car into the garage. I didn't know all this stuff was in here." She kicked a metal screw.

Alex stood as if glued to the floor, while Father turned his gaze on her.

"Uh, uh, well . . ." she stammered. "I, uh, thought I would try fixing my bicycle by myself. I mean, you know, I thought I'd surprise you. . . ."

Father stared at Alex in disbelief. "You opened the package with the bicycle parts?"

"Yes," Alex whispered.

"And all of the parts have just been run over by the car?" Father asked.

"Yes," Alex repeated.

"Barbara, I'd like to talk to Alex alone, please," Father said quietly.

Barbara left the garage. Alex stood in front of her father and cringed. She knew she had behaved wrongly and should be punished for it. But her father sank to

41

the garage floor and held his head in his hands. Finally, he spoke. "Firecracker, why didn't you wait for me?"

"I'm sorry, Dad," Alex felt hot tears sting her eyes. "I thought I could fix my bicycle myself."

"But now the parts are completely ruined," Father sighed. "We'll have to order another kit. It will have to be shipped again. It will take twice as long to fix your bicycle."

"I know," Alex wiped away tears with the back of her hand.

Father moved over to Alex and put his arms around her. "Sometimes it is very hard to have patience," he said, "especially when you want something badly. But patience is really good for you. It teaches you how to wait for the right time to do things. If we try to do things at the wrong time, we end up messing them up."

Father continued, "It's just the same as learning to trust your heavenly Father to pick the right times to give you His things."

"Oh," Alex nodded. "I never thought of it that way. Then patience is a real important thing to learn."

"Yes," Father said. "The Bible says we learn to trust God more by developing patience. It makes our faith strong."

"I'll try to do better next time, Dad," Alex leaned against her father and buried her head in his neck.

"I'm sure you will, Firecracker," Father hugged Alex. "I'm sure you will."

Amen.

 Food for Thought

Why is learning to have patience so important? What happened to Alex when she did not wait for her father to fix her bicycle? Patience is something God wants us to learn. We cannot be grown-up Christians without it.

In this story, the food from the Bible is:

___

Patience makes faith strong.

The Truth and Nothing But . . .

Jesus said to him, "I am the way,
and the truth, and the life; no one comes
to the Father, but through Me."
John 14:6 (NASB)

ALEX listened as Stephen gave his speech to the class. The more Alex heard, the angrier she became. She felt like pounding the desk with her fist as she heard Stephen's final remarks.

"So, as you can see, all religions are pretty much the same," Stephen concluded. "They all have a belief in a higher power, and they all say that people should be good. It doesn't really matter which religion a person follows. All religions worship God. They just do it in different ways."

Stephen's speech ended. He took his seat. Mrs. Hibbits, the teacher, walked to the front of the classroom.

"That was a very good speech, Stephen," Mrs. Hibbits told him. She held up her hands as some of the students groaned. Alex was one of them.

"I do not mean that I agree with what Stephen said," the teacher told the class. "I meant that he spoke very well. Because this is a public school, we are not allowed to discuss religion. If any of you were bothered by Stephen's speech, I suggest that you talk it over with your parents at home." The teacher glanced at the clock. "Class dismissed," she said just as the bell rang.

Alex quickly gathered her things together, and followed Stephen and two of his friends down the hall and out of the school building. Alex's friends, Janie, Julie, and Lorraine, ran to catch up with her.

"What do you mean saying all

religions are the same?" Alex almost shouted as she caught up with Stephen. "You know that isn't true. Christianity is the only true religion."

"It is not," Stephen retorted. "You're just saying that because it's the one you

practice. There are lots of different religions in the world. How can you say that yours is the one right religion?"

"Because it's the only one that teaches the truth!" Alex replied hotly.

"But everybody thinks their religion is the one true religion. My dad says that everybody has the right to their own opinion, and whatever a person believes is the truth. The truth can be different for each person."

"No," Alex insisted. "There can't be a whole bunch of different truths. There is only one truth, and Christianity is it!"

"Aw, you don't know what you're talking about," Stephen shoved past Alex.

"I do so!" Alex would have charged at Stephen, but her friends held her back.

"Alex, take it easy!" her friends held her tightly. They waited until Stephen was out of sight before they let go of Alex.

Alex walked home in a hurry. She was furious at Stephen and could hardly think of anything else.

When she got home, Alex went to her room to think about what she could say to Stephen. She decided to ask the one person who could help her.

"Dear Lord Jesus," Alex whispered, "please help Stephen understand that Christianity is the only right religion —that only You are the truth." She paused for a moment as a new thought entered her mind. "That's what I'll tell Stephen tomorrow," she said excitedly. "I'll tell him about You. Thanks, Lord. Amen."

The next day at morning recess, Alex felt a peaceful confidence as she confronted Stephen again. They met under a big oak tree that grew at the back of the playground. A crowd of children gathered around them.

"Christianity is the only true religion because it has Jesus. No other religions have Jesus," Alex calmly told Stephen.

Stephen frowned. "So what?" he asked. "Other religions have great people too. The Buddhists have Buddha, the Muslims have Muhammad, and the Hindus have Krishna. They think their prophets and holy men are just as good as Jesus."

"But they can't be," Alex said. "Jesus is the Son of God."

"Not everybody believes that," Stephen replied sourly. "What proof do you have that Jesus is the Son of God?"

Alex did not answer. She looked at her friends who were gathered around her. Why didn't they help her?

Alex thought for a minute then silently prayed, "Oh, Lord Jesus, please help me."

Suddenly, a little light flickered in Alex's mind, like a candle being lit in a dark room. Soon, the light spread until the whole room was bright and alive with the light.

"Of course!" Alex cried out loud. "That's it!"

She turned to Stephen and said, "I have proof that Jesus is the Son of God."

"What's that?" Stephen sneered.

"Jesus is the only One who was raised from the dead," Alex replied in a quiet but steady voice. "That was God's proof to the world to show us the difference between Jesus and the other men. No one else was raised from the dead."

The children grew quiet. No one said a word. Alex didn't know if Stephen would accept God's truth, but she felt peaceful knowing she had spoken it. The rest she knew she could leave up to God.

Amen.

 ## Food for Thought

What is God's proof that Jesus is His Son? Do you believe God's proof? The Bible says you can find God only through Jesus. There is no other way. If you ask Jesus, He will show you the true way.

In this story, the food from the Bible is:

_____

Jesus is the only way to God.

Cookie Splats!

Dear Friends, let us practice loving each other,
for love comes from God and those
who are loving and kind show that they are
the children of God.
I John 4:7a

MOM, there's nothing to do," Alex complained to her mother. "Janie's gone on vacation, Julie's at day camp, and Lorraine is visiting her grandma. There's no one to play with!"

"Yeah," Rudy broke in, "and my best friend, Jason, is gone away for a whole week!"

"Well," Mother looked from one to the other, "why don't you do something together?"

Alex frowned and eyed her little

brother. "I don't think so," she told Mother. "Rudy's a brat."

"I am not," Rudy shot back.

"Hmmpf!" Alex snorted and glared at Rudy.

"I'll tell you what," Mother had an idea. "I just bought a box of chocolate chip cookie mix. How would you two like to make some cookies?"

"Sure!" Rudy answered at once.

"You mean bake?" Alex cried indignantly. "With Rudy?"

"Oh, Alex, it's only a few chocolate chip cookies," Mother smiled. "It's not like I asked you to cook a whole dinner."

"Well, okay," Alex agreed reluctantly. "But you have to be careful and do what I say," she told Rudy as she picked up the box of cookie mix and read the back of the box.

Alex measured the ingredients and poured them into the bowl. She handed Rudy the bowl. "It's your turn to stir," she told him.

He attacked the job vigorously. "We

studied gravity in school last year," Rudy told Alex. "Our teacher said that whatever goes up must come down."

"That's right," Alex replied absently. She was busy searching in a bottom cupboard for a cookie sheet.

"Does that mean everything?" Rudy asked.

"Huh? What do you mean everything?" Alex asked, finally locating the cookie sheet and pulling it out of the cupboard.

"Does it mean that everything that goes up has to come back down?" Rudy asked again.

"Yeah, sure, everything," Alex mumbled, wondering why in the world Rudy was talking about gravity.

"It doesn't work for cookie dough," Rudy said matter-of-factly.

"Huh?" Alex frowned. "What doesn't work for cookie dough?"

"Gravity," Rudy replied. "Gravity doesn't work for cookie dough. See!" He pointed at the ceiling.

Slowly, Alex raised her eyes. She

gasped! A flattened ball of cookie dough stuck to the ceiling right above Rudy's head.

"Rudy!" Alex cried. "You threw cookie dough on the ceiling?!"

"I just wanted to see if it would come down like you said," Rudy explained.

"But . . . but . . . " Alex sputtered.

"It's fun! Watch!" Before Alex could stop him, Rudy flung another hunk of dough up into the air. SPLAT! It hit the ceiling and stuck.

"Rudy, cut it out," Alex hissed. "We're gonna get in trouble."

"You oughta try it," Rudy laughed. "It's lots of fun!"

Alex sighed. She looked from the bowl to the ceiling and back to the bowl again. Maybe she would try it. After all, there were already two balls stuck to the ceiling. How much harm could one more do?

"Okay," Alex finally grinned. She took the spoon from Rudy and put a chunk of dough on the end of it. Holding the spoon out in front of her, Alex flipped

her wrist, sending the cookie dough SPLAT! to the ceiling.

"This is great!" Alex cried. "I just gotta do another one." She put more dough on the spoon and flung it to the ceiling.

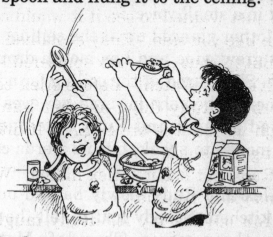

Rudy got out another spoon and joined Alex. They had a great time covering the ceiling with cookie dough. Before they knew it, there was no dough left in the bowl. It was all on the ceiling.

"Isn't it beautiful?" Alex asked Rudy as they stood back to admire the once all-white ceiling. Now it was decorated with globs of brown cookie dough and dark chocolate chips.

"How are the cookies coming?" Mother asked as she suddenly appeared in the doorway. "And what are you two looking at?"

"Uh, you don't want to know," replied Alex in a small voice.

Mother glanced up at the ceiling. Her eyes grew wide and her mouth dropped open. She stared at the ceiling for a long moment. Then she lowered her eyes and stared at Alex and Rudy. She opened her mouth to speak, but no words came out.

Alex and Rudy slowly backed out of the kitchen. Nobody had to tell them to go to their rooms. They left Mother standing in the kitchen and crept upstairs. They did not see or hear from Mother until Father came home.

"Alex and Rudy, we will use your allowance money to buy some paint," Father told them sternly. "You will also spend the weekend helping us scrape off the cookie dough and repaint the ceiling."

"Okay," Alex sighed. "We're really sorry about messing up the ceiling. It's just that it was so much fun, we couldn't stop."

"Yeah, I guess we got carried away," Rudy added.

"You can say that again!" Mother replied.

"You may not think it was so much fun after you have spent some time cleaning it up," Father told them.

"Yeah," Alex nodded and sighed. She thought for a moment, then told her parents, "Well, there's one good thing about it."

"What's that?" they frowned.

"Rudy and I found out that doing things together can be lots of fun!"

Amen.

Were Alex and Rudy eager to spend time together? Even though throwing cookie dough on the ceiling was a wrong thing to do, Alex found that she enjoyed doing things with her brother. What are some things you could do with your sisters or brothers?

In this story, the food from the Bible is:

Love your sisters and brothers.

Awesome Anger

It is better to be slow-tempered than famous.
Proverbs 16:32a

BUT I already turned in my social studies report," Alex told her teacher. "I turned it in early."

"Alex, I have checked and checked through all my papers, and I do not have your report," Mrs. Hibbits replied.

"But I laid it on your desk last week," Alex said.

"Alex, I don't remember seeing it at all," answered the teacher. "You will have to do another one by tomorrow."

"But that's not fair!" Alex exclaimed.

She felt her face turn red and her muscles tense.

"Alex, this discussion has ended," said Mrs. Hibbits in a no-arguing tone of voice.

Alex turned and stomped her way back to her desk. "Brussels sprouts!" she fumed. "It took me two whole days to write that report, and now I have to do it all over again in one night." Alex looked across the aisle to see Eddie Thompson grinning at her. Alex glared back at him.

"What's the matter, Alex?" Eddie hissed. "Couldn't you get out of doing the social studies report?"

"Yeah, Alex, too bad Mrs. Hibbits didn't fall for your story about turning the report in early," teased Joshua Barton, one of Eddie's friends.

"She probably didn't even turn it in at all," chuckled Eddie.

"I did so!" cried Alex angrily. She picked up a book and threw it across the aisle at Eddie.

BLAM! Eddie ducked and the book

hit the wall behind him.

"Alex," Mrs. Hibbits said sternly, "pick up that book and sit down immediately."

Alex picked up her book and sat down in her chair. She laid her head down on the desk and ignored the boys. Things were not going well at all today. She wished she had not come to school.

Finally, the morning recess bell rang. Alex stomped outside with Janie and her friends. She fussed and fumed about the loss of her social studies report.

"What's the matter, Alex? Lose something?" Eddie and Joshua laughed as they ran past the girls.

"You birdbrains!" Alex shouted. Before her friends could stop her, Alex took off after the boys. She caught up with Joshua and pushed him to the ground.

SHREEEEE! The playground teacher blew her whistle. She marched angrily over to Alex. "We do not allow that kind of roughhousing on the playground. You will stand beside me for the rest of recess."

Alex knew better than to argue. She

stood beside the teacher while the boys laughed and the girls shook their heads.

That afternoon, Alex did her best to control her temper. She did not look at or speak to anyone. She refused to answer any questions in class. Finally, by the end of the day, Alex had a raging headache. She trudged home and told her mother all about her terrible day at school.

"I'm sorry you had such a bad day, Alex," Mother replied, "but you know what? Many unfair things happen in life. We just have to learn to make the best of them."

"But Eddie and Joshua kept teasing

me, and I was the one who got in trouble! And now I have to write a social studies report that I already did!" Alex cried.

"You got in trouble because you threw a book at Eddie and pushed Joshua down on the playground," Mother reminded her. "As for the social studies report, I'm sorry you have to write it again, but there's nothing else to do."

Alex stomped up to her bedroom. She grabbed some paper and pencils. She got out the encyclopedias and began working on the report. However, the more she worked, the more angry she became. Finally, she slammed the books shut and went to lie down on her bed.

It's not fair! It's not fair! The words screamed through her mind. She tried to shut off the angry thoughts, but they kept echoing around and around inside her head.

"If I could stop being so angry and settle down, I could get the report done," Alex told herself. Tears of frustration filled her eyes. Finally, she turned to the one person who could help her.

"Dear Lord Jesus," she prayed, "please help me to stop being so angry. I need Your help. Amen."

Almost immediately, Alex felt better. She had turned her problem over to someone bigger and stronger who would take care of it for her. She did not have to worry about it anymore. Alex lay still on her bed and let her thoughts drift together until she felt herself float off to sleep.

When Alex awoke, she was surprised to see that her room was dark. A light tapping noise sounded on the door.

"Hello, Sleepyhead," smiled Mother as she walked into the room. "It's time for dinner."

"Already?" Alex yawned. "You mean I slept that long?"

"It seemed like you needed it," Mother replied. "You looked so peaceful, I didn't want to wake you."

"Peaceful?" Alex repeated slowly. That was funny! How could she be so peaceful when she had been so angry before?

"That's funny," Alex told her mother. "I asked the Lord to help me stop being angry, and then I fell asleep. Now I do feel peaceful."

"And how do you feel about Eddie, Joshua, and Mrs. Hibbits?" Mother asked with a smile.

"Well, I guess Mrs. Hibbits is human, and all human beings make mistakes," Alex replied, "so I guess I can forgive her." Alex grinned, then said, "I don't know about the boys, though. They don't seem very human to me!"

"Oh, Alex!" Mother laughed.

"But I still don't want to do the report over again," Alex frowned.

"I know," Mother said. "Come on. Let's eat. Maybe after dinner, I can help you with the report."

Alex and Mother went downstairs and joined the rest of the family for dinner. They had just finished when the telephone rang.

"Hello?" said Father. He listened a moment and then passed the phone to Alex. "It's your teacher, Mrs. Hibbits," he whispered with a puzzled look on his face.

"Uh, hello?" Alex said. She listened carefully to her teacher's words. A big smile spread across her face. "Oh, that's okay," she said into the phone. "Thank you for calling." Alex hung up.

"Well, what was that all about?" Father and Mother wanted to know.

"Mrs. Hibbits told me she just found my social studies report in a stack of her papers at home," Alex told them with a big grin. "I don't need to do the report over after all!"

"Well, how about that?" Mother asked with a knowing smile. "Now wasn't it strange that you fell asleep when you did? Otherwise, you would have spent all this time rewriting a report that you didn't need to rewrite after all."

"Yeah, funny thing," Alex thought it over. "That must have been the Lord. He removed my anger and put me to sleep so I wouldn't do the report over for nothing. Brussels sprouts, the Lord sure takes good care of me!"

Father and Mother laughed, "He sure does, Alex."

Amen.

 ## Food for Thought

Why was Alex so angry? What happened when she let her anger run out of control? What happened when she prayed about it? How did the Lord help Alex deal with her terrible day?

In this story, the food from the Bible is:

Forgive, don't stay angry.

Miracles!

I love the Lord because he hears
my prayers and answers them.
Psalm 116:1

HEY, Mom!" Alex hollered down the stairs. "Have you seen my tape player?"

"No, I haven't seen it for a while," Mother called from the kitchen. "Have you checked in your room?"

"Yeah, we've searched the whole house and can't find it anywhere," Alex wailed. "Janie and I want to listen to our school band tape."

"Well," Mother came to the bottom of the stairs, "why don't you try Rudy's room, Barbara's room, and the basement?"

"But we've already looked everywhere," Alex moaned.

Mother suddenly smiled at Alex and Janie. "I have an idea," she told the girls. "Alex, do you remember what I did when I couldn't find the keys to the car the other day?"

"Oh, yeah," Alex's face brightened. "You asked the Lord to find them and He did!"

"That's right," Mother nodded. "He showed me right where those keys were. Why don't you try asking the Lord to help you find the tape player?"

"Okay," Alex and Janie said eagerly. They closed their eyes and bowed their heads.

"Dear Lord Jesus," Alex prayed out loud, "please help us find the tape player. We pray in Your name. Amen."

"Now what do we do?" Janie wanted to know.

"Well, we kinda look around and let Him lead us to it," Alex answered.

The girls walked around the house, scanning the rooms, looking behind doors and under furniture. Alex walked through the kitchen and glanced out the back door window. Her eyes immediately fixed on the big oak tree standing toward the back of the yard. Alex halted in mid-stride.

"Brussels sprouts!" she cried. "Mom! Janie! Come here quick! I know where it is!"

Mother and Janie hurried to Alex's side.

"I'm sure the tape player is in the tree house," Alex told them. "I remember now that Rudy and I were playing music tapes up there."

"Well, let's go see!" said Janie. She and Alex ran to the tree. Mother followed them across the yard and stood at the base of the tree while Alex and Janie climbed up to the tree house. The girls rushed inside. There, in the center of the room, on a little round table, sat the tape player.

"Wow!" Alex and Janie breathed together. They looked at one another with shining eyes. God had just given them a miracle!

"It's here!" Alex called down to Mother.

Mother smiled. "You need to thank the Lord for finding your tape player," she told the girls.

"Thank You, Lord Jesus," Alex and Janie said together.

Their happiness, however, was short-lived, for in the next moment Alex checked the basket of tapes and discovered that the band music tape was missing.

"Hey, Mom," Alex shouted down from the tree. "My band tape's not here!"

"Oh, Alex, for heaven's sake!" Mother threw up her hands and went back inside the house.

Alex and Janie looked at one another.

"Do you think the Lord would mind if we asked Him to find the tape too?" Janie asked Alex in a low voice.

"I guess not," Alex replied. The two girls knelt down beside the table. "Dear Lord Jesus," Alex prayed, "would You please help us find the band tape? I'm sorry I lost it too. We pray in Your name. Amen."

As Alex and Janie lugged the tape player down from the tree house, Alex suddenly hooted with joy. "Brussels sprouts! I just remembered that the band tape is inside the pocket of my raincoat. I took it to Lorraine's house last Friday. It was raining so I wore my raincoat."

The girls raced to the big hall closet by the front door. Alex yanked out her raincoat and felt in one of the pockets. Triumphantly, she pulled out the music tape!

"Awesome!" Janie cried with a grin. Once again, the girls thanked the Lord for His help.

Later that afternoon, after Janie had gone home, Alex decided to finish reading her library book. It was due back in the school library the next day. After searching her room, however, she could not find the book. Finally, she lay down on her bed and covered her face with her hands.

"Dear Lord Jesus," Alex prayed desperately, "I know I've already asked You to find two things for me today, but I just gotta find my library book. I'll be in big trouble if I don't find it. Please help me find just this one more thing today. I pray in Your name. Amen."

Alex got up off her bed and began walking through the house in search of the missing book. She looked in every room, but it was nowhere to be found. She did not mention the lost book to anyone. She especially did not want her mother to know she had lost something again, particularly something as important as a library book.

By dinnertime, Alex was extremely upset. There was just no other place to look for the book.

"I guess I asked the Lord to help me too many times today," Alex told herself. "He's probably tired of helping a dumb kid who always loses things."

After dinner, Father asked Alex to go with him to the hardware store.

"What's the matter, Firecracker?" Father asked Alex, using his nickname for her, as they made their way to the store. "You didn't seem yourself tonight at dinner."

Alex sighed. She told her father all about her day of losing things and how the Lord had helped her find them again.

"But He won't help me find my library book," Alex sniffed. "I think He's tired of helping me."

"I don't think the Lord ever gets tired of helping His children," Father said as he stopped the car. He pulled Alex close and hugged her. "Just give Him time. The book must be in a very strange place."

"You can say that again," Alex frowned.

"Come on, Firecracker," Father rumpled her hair, "it's not the end of the world. Let's go into the hardware store."

As Father climbed out of the car, the keys to the car dropped from his hand and fell under the car seat.

"I'll get them," Alex volunteered. She lay upside down on the seat and stuck her head underneath it.

"Here they are," she said, picking up the keys from the floor of the car. "Hey,

wait a minute!" she suddenly cried. "There's something else under here." She reached further under the seat and tugged. Out came the missing library book!

"I found it! I found it!" Alex shouted. "It was under the seat all this time."

"I guess the Lord was just waiting for you to go to the store with me," Father grinned.

"Yeah, and He was waiting for you to drop your keys," added Alex.

"It's a good thing I'm such a butterfingers," chuckled Father. Alex laughed with him.

"Thank You, Lord!" she cried. "Thank You for answering all of my prayers!"

Amen.

 Food for Thought

What three things did the Lord find for Alex? The Bible tells us to keep praying for the things we need. God never gets tired of hearing our prayers. What do you need His help with today?

In this story, the food from the Bible is:

God hears and answers prayer.

76

Scarface

Little children, let us stop just saying we love people; let us really love them, and show it by our actions.
I John 3:18

UH-OH, here she comes!" the girls in the lunchroom cried.

"Shhhhh!" Alex hissed. "She'll hear you!"

The girls turned and watched as Sarah, the new girl in school, walked slowly to their lunch table. She shyly glanced at the girls, then quickly took a place at the end of the table by herself. The other girls giggled.

Alex frowned and watched as Sarah ducked her head and silently began eating her lunch. Giggles, whispers, and the name "Scarface" ran up and down the table. A silent tear rolled down Sarah's face.

Angrily, Alex stood up from the table. She could no longer stand the rude behavior of her friends. She left the group of girls and marched down to sit at the end of the table—right across from Sarah.

"Hi, Sarah," Alex spoke to the new girl.

Sarah looked up at Alex gratefully. "Hi," she answered shyly.

"Uh, my name is Alex, in case you forgot," Alex said with a smile.

"Oh, yeah, sorry," Sarah replied. "I'm having a hard time remembering names."

"That's okay, I understand," Alex replied. "After all, you've only been here two days, right?"

"Yeah, that's right," Sarah said. There was an awkward silence. Alex could hear the other girls snicker. She decided to ignore them.

"Well, uh, Sarah," Alex began again, "we have recess right after lunch. Do you want to do something together?"

"Sure!" Sarah cried and leaned forward so eagerly that she dumped over her milk carton. The spilled milk covered her tray.

The table full of girls erupted with laughter so loud that all heads in the cafeteria turned to look at them. Sarah's eyes filled with tears. She hid her face in her hands.

Alex took Sarah by the arm and led her out to the playground. They sat down on two swings. Sarah wiped her eyes and tried to smile at Alex.

"Don't worry about those dopey girls," Alex told her. "They can be really rude sometimes."

Sarah and Alex swung for a while. Alex watched the other girls come out onto the playground and climb the jungle gym. The jungle gym was too close to the swings for Alex. She and Sarah got up and walked away.

"Hey, do you wanna play tetherball?" Alex asked Sarah.

"Well, I have never played it before," Sarah answered, "but I'll try it."

"Okay, wait here," Alex told her. "I'll get the ball from the playground teacher."

Alex ran off to find Mr. Carpenter, one of the teachers on playground duty. She found him supervising a game of basketball. He was so involved in the basketball game, it took Alex a few minutes to make him understand what she wanted. As she turned to follow him across the playground, she looked back to where she had left Sarah. Alex suddenly gasped and raised her hand to her mouth in fear. The mob of rude girls had moved to surround Sarah!

Although Alex could not hear them, she was certain the girls were saying mean things to Sarah. As Alex watched, Sarah slowly moved toward the fence at the back of the playground. The girls followed her. Suddenly, Sarah broke from the group and ran straight for the fence. She leaped onto the fence and was over it before anyone could stop her.

"Wait! Stop! Sarah!" Alex screamed at the top of her lungs. She ran as fast as she could, but before she reached the fence, Sarah darted into the street that ran behind the school. Tires screeched and brakes squealed as the oncoming cars tried to stop. Alex heard a sickening thud as one of the cars slid sideways into another car that was going in the opposite direction. Alex raised her hands to her face in horror. Sarah was no longer in sight. She had fallen down between the cars.

"Oh, God!" Alex cried out loud. "Please make her be all right!"

Later that afternoon, Alex and her mother sat in the waiting room at the hospital. Soon, some of the teachers began to arrive. Finally, to Alex's disgust, the group of girls responsible for Sarah's accident filed into the waiting room. They came one by one with their parents. All of the girls hung their heads in shame and did not look at Alex.

Some time later, Sarah's mother came out to the waiting room. "Sarah will be all right," she told the crowd of anxious people. "She has a broken leg and several cuts and scrapes. She'll have to stay in the hospital tonight, but she can go home tomorrow."

Everyone breathed a sigh of relief.

"Sarah has told me that the girls in her class made fun of the scars she has on her face," Sarah's mother continued sadly. "Sarah has those scars because she was abused as a young child. My husband and I have recently adopted Sarah and will make every effort to heal her physical and emotional problems."

There was a heavy silence in the waiting room. As Alex glanced around, she noticed that there was not a dry eye in the room. The girls wept openly.

Sarah's mother left the room. Soon, Sarah was moved into the hallway next to the waiting room. Alex could see her from the doorway. She was sitting in a wheelchair, and a bright lavender cast covered her right leg. Alex ran out to see her.

"Hi, Alex!" Sarah said brightly. "I'm all right. Thanks for coming to see me. Do you like my cast?"

"Yeah, it's neat," Alex replied with a smile. "I really like the color." Her smile faded as the other girls walked slowly over to Sarah and stood in front of her.

"Sarah, we are really sorry for the mean things we said to you," Elizabeth spoke first for the group.

"Yes, we were wrong to say them," added Mary Jane. "We'd like to be your friends."

"Yes, please forgive us!" cried out several of the girls at once.

A smile crept slowly over Sarah's face. "Okay," she said shyly. "Let's be friends."

Alex breathed a big sigh of relief. Everyone began to talk and giggle at once. The hall was suddenly filled with such happiness that Alex just shook her head in wonder. Things had worked out even better than she had hoped. In fact, it was an absolute miracle! Alex smiled to herself. Only the Lord could have turned this tragedy into something so wonderful.

"Thanks, Lord," Alex prayed. "Thanks for taking care of Sarah and making things turn out so well."

Amen.

Why did the girls make fun of Sarah? How was Alex different? The Bible says we must love all people. It doesn't matter what they look like. How did Alex show God's love to Sarah? How can you show God's love today?

In this story, the food from the Bible is:

Love people by your actions.

True Blue

If you love someone you will be loyal to him
no matter what the cost.
I Corinthians 13:7a

I'M gonna make it through the inner tube this time," Alex called to the children on the dock. "Watch me!

"COWABUNGA!" she cried as she jumped off the dock into the cold lake water below. This time, both her feet went through the hole in the big black inner tube.

"Hooray for cousin Alex!" shouted a blond-haired teenage boy. He treaded water below the dock and held the inner tube in place for the younger children.

When Alex came up for air, he grabbed her and turned her upside down.

"Blaffpptt!" Alex spit lake water out of her mouth. "Cousin Jackie, I'm gonna get you for that!"

Alex grabbed hold of Jackie and tried to dunk him. The other children plunged into the water to help Alex.

"Help!" Jackie shouted as children of all ages leaped on his shoulders. "Time out!" he cried and shook himself free of the younger children. He climbed the ladder to the dock and sat down by Alex's older sister, Barbara.

Alex rolled her eyes and sighed. She was afraid her favorite cousin, Jackie, was starting to like her dopey blonde sister, Barbara, better than her.

Alex's family had come to the lake for a family reunion. Aunts, uncles, and cousins were there from all over the country. The most fun-loving cousin and Alex's favorite was Jackie. Even though they were years apart in age, Alex and Jackie had always been close in spirit.

This summer, however, things seemed different between them. Instead of playing ball with Alex, Jackie sat on the dock with Barbara. He wouldn't even go waterskiing without Barbara in the boat.

Alex sighed. She and Jackie used to have such good times together. She had looked forward to the reunion at the lake all summer. Now it was ruined.

That night at a family barbecue on the outside terrace, Alex tried one more time to capture Jackie's attention. She boldly strode over to where Jackie and Barbara were sitting in a corner of the patio and shoved a bright blue balloon filled with water under Jackie's nose.

"Jackie," Alex said, "they're having games out on the terrace. Would you be my partner in the water balloon toss?"

"Great! A water balloon toss!" Jackie grinned. "Come on, Barbara, let's go!"

Without a word to Alex, the two teenagers ran off. Alex stared after them for a moment. Then, she angrily smashed the water balloon to the ground.

"That does it!" Alex cried out loud. "I never want to see him again!"

With tears streaming down her face, Alex ran off the patio and onto the beach. She did not care in what direction she moved. She ran past the dock and neighboring houses. She ran further along the shore until finally she climbed a giant hill. She stopped suddenly at the top of it. A body of water blocked her way.

Frowning at the water, Alex suddenly realized that she was on top of the dam that separated the small private lake from a larger lake. She stopped and stared at the water as it moved across the dam. It looked shallow enough to cross. Taking a deep breath, Alex stepped over a low concrete wall and onto the dam.

The water was about knee level. It was icy cold. Soon her legs and bare feet began to feel numb as the cold water rushed around her. Alex stepped gingerly as she pushed her way across the dam. She fought to keep her balance as the rush of water picked up speed in the middle of the dam. Suddenly, Alex stepped on something soft and squishy.

"YIKES!" she hollered, thinking she might have stepped on a snake. She gave a small jump backward, lost her balance, and tumbled into the water.

"HELP!" she cried as she plunged over the edge of the dam and into the foamy water below.

Alex hit the water hard. She sank so deep in the water, that for a few minutes, she could not figure out which way was up. When she did come up for air, the churning water almost made it impossible to breathe.

Gasping, Alex glanced frantically around. Seeing a nearby boulder, she paddled over to it. Wrapping both arms around it, Alex floated beside the boulder and rested her aching body.

Darkness fell and still Alex clutched the boulder. Her entire body felt frozen and numb. Alex tried to be brave, but fear mounted inside her. She could no longer see the dam. Inky blackness

surrounded her. Only the heavens shone brightly above her.

Alex raised her eyes to look at the shining stars. "Oh, Lord Jesus," she moaned, "please help me."

As if in answer, a sudden bobbing light shone from the top of the dam. "Alex? Is that you?" called a voice.

"HELP!" Alex shrieked in answer. "I'm down here! In the water!"

The light flashed in her direction. "Hold on, Alex! I'm coming!" the voice called again.

Alex watched the light at the top of the dam bob lower and lower as if it were hopping its way down the dam and over the water. It moved closer and closer to her until finally Alex could see the person who swam toward her. It was Jackie!

"Thank God I found you!" Jackie exclaimed. He gently pulled her toward him and away from the boulder. He then turned Alex on her back and pulled her to shore. He lifted her in his arms.

"How'd you ever find me?" Alex asked as he walked slowly back to the beach.

"Well, that was kinda funny," Jackie replied in a low voice. "We looked everywhere for you and couldn't find you. Then, just a few minutes ago, I asked God to help me find you, and right away I heard you cry for help!"

"Brussels sprouts! That is funny! I had just prayed to God for help right before I saw your light!" Alex cried happily.

"I guess we asked Him for help at the same time," Jackie chuckled. "I'm sure glad He answered."

"Me too," Alex sighed. She was safe now, but as her fear disappeared, she suddenly remembered why she had run away in the first place.

Jackie must have thought of it too, for he said, "Uh, Alex, I'm really sorry I didn't do the water balloon toss with you tonight. I guess I have been kinda ignoring you."

"That's okay," Alex sniffed. "I guess you started liking Barbara instead of me."

"That's not true," Jackie answered. "I like you both. I just didn't realize how much I had been ignoring you." He gave Alex a big brother-like squeeze. "You are still my friend, and it was wrong of me not to pay attention to you. Will you forgive me?"

"Okay," Alex grinned.

"We'll go waterskiing tomorrow, okay?" asked Jackie.

"Without Barbara?" Alex asked eagerly.

"Without Barbara," Jackie smiled. "Can we still be favorite cousins, loyal to the end?"

"True blue forever!" Alex cried happily. She gazed up at the twinkling stars. "Thanks, Lord," she prayed silently. "Thanks for rescuing me, and thanks that Jackie and I are friends again."

Amen.

 **Food for Thought**

How did Jackie hurt Alex? Was he a loyal friend? It's important to be loyal to our friends even when we make new ones. By being loyal to our friends, we learn to be loyal to God.

In this story, the food from the Bible is:

Be loyal to your friends.

Turtle Trouble

When God's children are in need, you be the
one to help them out.
Romans 12:13a

ONE summer afternoon, Alex stretched
out on Father's backyard hammock. She
had a book in one hand and a can of ice
cold root beer in the other. She had just
pitched a close game of softball, and she
was tired.

"Ahhhhhh!" Alex sighed contentedly
as she lay her head back on a pillow. She
took a sip of root beer and opened her
book.

"ALEX!" Rudy suddenly screamed,
running up behind the hammock with

his best friend, Jason.

The loud noise caught Alex off guard. Jerking upright and turning to stare at Rudy, Alex lost her balance. The hammock flipped completely upside down, spilling Alex, the book, and the can of root beer to the ground.

"Alex, are you all right?" Rudy asked. He and Jason squatted down on either side of Alex and peered into her face.

"Rudy," Alex moaned, "if you ever do that again, I'm gonna pulverize you!"

"Uh, sorry, Alex," Rudy apologized, "but we need your help. It's an emergency!"

"Yeah," Jason agreed. "Clementine's lost!"

"Brussels sprouts!" Alex scowled. "I got dumped out of the hammock for a dumb old turtle?"

"Clementine's not a dumb old turtle!" Jason objected.

"Alex, we need your help," Rudy cut in quickly. "We can't find Clementine anywhere. We turned our backs for a few minutes, and she disappeared right out of Jason's backyard. Please help us find her."

Alex stared from one boy to the other. "Oh, all right," she sighed.

The boys showed Alex the last place they had seen Clementine. Alex and the boys searched carefully, each taking a different section of the yard. It was easy to overlook a turtle in the grass, even a large snapping turtle like Clementine.

They did not give up the search until Mother called them inside. With tears in his eyes, Jason waved good-bye. Alex and Rudy walked slowly home. They felt sorry for Jason.

"Jason's really sad," Rudy told Alex.

"I know," Alex replied.

"Where do you think Clementine went?" asked Rudy.

"I don't know," said Alex.

"We just gotta find her for Jason," Rudy insisted.

"There's nothing more we can do," Alex told him. "We looked everywhere."

"Maybe we could we say a prayer for

Clementine," Rudy suggested. "Maybe the Lord would help us find her."

"Great idea," Alex agreed. She and Rudy stood close together and bowed their heads. "Dear Lord Jesus," Alex prayed, "please help us find Clementine so that Jason will not be sad anymore. We pray in Your name. Amen."

Later that evening, about bedtime, Alex went to the back door to call in her dog, T-Bone, and her cat, Tuna.

"T-BONE! TUNA!" Alex called out the back door. "TIME TO COME IN!"

"WOOF!" T-Bone replied, but he did not come running. Neither did the cat.

"T-BONE! TUNA!" Alex called again. "COME HERE!"

"WOOF! WOOF!" T-Bone sounded excited.

"MEOW!" Tuna responded, but neither animal would come to Alex.

Alex flicked on the yard lights. She could see both animals out by the swing set. They were prancing around and around in excited circles.

"Hey, Mom! Dad! Something weird's going on in the backyard," Alex called to her parents.

"It looks like something is out there," Mother said, as she, Father, and Rudy came to stand beside Alex.

"Well, we'll just have to see," Father said as he grabbed a flashlight and stepped outside. He slowly advanced toward the animals.

All at once, Mother, Alex, and Rudy were startled to hear Father laugh. "Alex, get a box and come out here," he called.

Alex grabbed a box from the garage

and hurried outside. Mother and Rudy followed.

"What did you find?" Alex asked Father.

"This!" he chuckled and held up a large snapping turtle.

"Clementine!" Alex and Rudy cried together.

"We gotta take Clementine over to Jason's house right away," Alex and Rudy told their parents.

"It's awfully late," Mother objected.

"But I know Jason," Rudy told her. "He won't be able to sleep all night without Clementine!"

"Don't tell me he sleeps with that dumb turtle!" Alex exclaimed.

"Of course not," Rudy made a face, "but Clementine sleeps in a cage beside his bed. Jason says he goes to sleep listening to Clementine's scratching noises."

Mother, Father, and Alex laughed.

"It's not really that late," Alex told her mother. "It's only a little after nine."

"Okay, okay," Mother gave in. "Take

Clementine over to Jason. But don't stay and talk. Come right back."

Alex and Rudy quickly carried Clementine across the yard to Jason's house.

Jason's father met them at the door. "What are you two doing out so late?" he asked.

"We found Clementine!" Alex and Rudy announced. They proudly handed Jason's father the box with the turtle inside.

"That's wonderful!" Jason's father exclaimed. He called Jason to the door.

"What's going on?" Jason asked.

"I believe this belongs to you," his father said and handed him the box.

"OH, BOY!" Jason shouted when he saw Clementine. "Where'd you find her?"

"T-Bone and Tuna found her," Alex giggled. She and Rudy told Jason and his father about Clementine's rescue. Then they said good-bye and hurried back home.

As Alex got into bed that night, she

remembered how happy Jason looked when he saw Clementine. His face had shone with delight. To make another person that happy was worth all the trouble in the world—even falling out of a hammock!

As she knelt beside her bed, Alex added to the end of her prayers, "Thank You, Lord Jesus, for helping us find Clementine for Jason."

Amen.

 Food for Thought

How did Alex try to help Jason? Was Alex glad that she did? Why do you think it is important to help other people?

In this story, the food from the Bible is:

Helping others is important.

102

A Tall, Dark Stranger

You have advisors by the ton—your astrologers and stargazers, who try to tell you what the future holds. But they are as useless as dried grass burning in the fire.
Isaiah 47:13, 14a

NOW, girls," Mother said to Alex and Janie as they entered the Kingswood Shopping Mall. "You may shop together for an hour. Meet me at the fountain on the lower level."

"Okay," Alex and Janie agreed. They took off at a fast pace. Finally, their mothers had agreed to let them shop on their own for a whole hour. Of course, Alex's mother would be in the mall at the same time.

"Where do ya wanna go?" Janie asked.

"How about the bookstore?" Alex suggested, pointing to a nearby shop. "We can look at the comic books."

"Okay," Janie nodded.

After entering the bookstore, Alex pulled out a large book with a picture of the cat Garfield on the cover. Suddenly Janie said, "Alex, I forgot to tell you that I read my horoscope for today in the newspaper and . . ."

"Janie!" Alex exclaimed before her friend could finish. "You're not supposed to do that!"

"Huh?" Janie looked confused. "Why not?"

"Because Christians aren't supposed to mess with astrology. It says so in the Bible," replied Alex.

"Oh," Janie frowned. "Well, I was really just reading the comics, and the horoscopes were on the same page. Anyway, my horoscope said to beware of a tall, dark man!"

"Oh, Janie, that's ridiculous!" Alex snickered.

Just then, someone tried to squeeze past Alex and Janie in the narrow aisle. The girls looked up. Standing above them was a tall man with dark skin and dark curly hair.

"Ahhhhhhh!" Janie cried. She dropped the book she was looking at and ran down the aisle and out of the store.

"Janie!" Alex hollered. She quickly returned the book to the shelf and ran after her friend. She found Janie outside the bookstore, crouched on a bench behind a potted tree.

"Alex," Janie whispered, peeking

around the tree, "did you see that man? Do you think he was the one in the horoscope? He was certainly tall and dark!"

"No," Alex replied with a big sigh, "I do not even believe in horoscopes, and neither should you. Come on, you are going to ruin our shopping day if you keep acting like this!"

"Okay, Alex, I'm sorry," Janie said, her cheeks red with embarrassment. She climbed out from behind the potted tree.

"That's okay, Janie," Alex patted her friend's shoulder. "Let's just have fun today and not worry about things, okay?"

"Okay," Janie agreed. "Let's go into the candy store."

"Great idea!" Alex responded.

The girls skipped hand in hand down the mall to the candy store. They walked inside and stood looking at the rows and rows of plastic bins, each one full of candy.

The girls had a hard time deciding which kind of candy to get. Finally, Alex chose grape and root beer taffy, while Janie picked candy hearts.

They filled plastic bags with the candy and went to stand in line at the cash register. To Alex's amusement, a tall, dark-haired man also came to the register. He stood in line right behind Janie.

Alex nudged her friend and began to giggle. Soon Janie joined in Alex's laughter. People in the store stared at the girls as they nearly doubled over with a severe case of the giggles.

Red-faced and embarrassed, Alex reached the cashier. She pulled money out of her back pocket and quickly paid for her candy. Janie took a little longer to pay as she balanced candy, a purse, and money. Finally, the two girls rushed out of the store into the mall, laughing with relief.

"Hey!" a loud voice suddenly called after them.

Alex and Janie turned to see a man wave at them.

"Oh, Alex, it's the tall, dark man from

the candy store!" Janie cried. "What'll we do?"

Alex frowned as she stared back at the man. She did not believe a word of Janie's horoscope. Still, she knew better than to talk to strangers in the mall.

"I don't know," Alex replied. She looked at her watch. "Uh-oh, it's time to meet Mom!"

"But we'll have to go back past that man to get to your mom," Janie said frantically. "And he's coming closer!"

"Run for it, Janie!" Alex shouted. She dashed past the man and punched him in the stomach as hard as she could.

"Ugh!" the man doubled over in pain as Janie slipped by him and ran up the mall with Alex.

"Wait! Stop!" the man called after them.

Alex and Janie did not stop but ran straight to Alex's mother.

"Alex? Janie? What is the matter?" Mother cried.

"There's a man chasing us!" Alex gasped. Alex and Janie darted behind

Mother's back as the tall man with dark hair hurried up to them.

"May I help you?" Mother frowned at the man.

"Excuse me," the man gasped, out of breath. "I mean no harm. I believe one of the young ladies dropped this five-dollar bill out of her purse at the candy store."

"What? Who, me?" Janie cried. Her face turned bright red as she opened her purse and discovered that the five-dollar bill was hers.

"Uh, thank you," Janie stammered as the man handed her the money.

"Uh, I'm sorry I punched you back there," Alex apologized to the man. "I thought you were after us."

"That's okay," the man smiled. "I understand."

"Alex," Mother frowned as she watched the man walk away, "would you please tell me what is going on?"

"Well, Mom, you see, Janie read her horoscope for today and . . ."

Alex and Janie told Mother all that

had happened. Mother laughed so hard that she had to sit down on a bench.

"Janie," Mother finally said, "I hope that you will not pay attention to any more horoscopes." Mother smiled. "Horoscopes are dangerous," she told the girls. "As you found out today, they are not truthful. But many times, they come just close enough to the truth that people start believing in them. Then people rely on their horoscopes instead of on God. The Bible warns us to stay away from astrology."

Alex and Janie nodded.

"Do you girls still want to shop by yourselves?" Mother asked.

"Sure!" Alex and Janie cried together.

"Janie," Mother asked another question, "what are you going to do when you see a tall dark stranger?"

"Smile," Janie replied and ran off down the mall with Alex.

Amen.

Food for Thought

How did Janie's horoscope get Alex and Janie in trouble? Was Janie's horoscope right? Why should we stay away from astrology and all other forms of the occult?

In this story, the food from the Bible is:

Trust God, not astrology.

A Mustard Seed Moment

If you have faith as a mustard seed,
you shall say to this mountain, "Move from
here to there," and it shall move;
and nothing shall be impossible to you.
Matthew 17:20b (NASB)

"THIS place looks scary!" Janie whispered to Alex as their bus moved slowly down an inner-city street. The bus turned and inched its way into a narrow, circular driveway. It finally came to a stop in front of a large, broken-down brick building covered with straggling ivy.

"We have arrived at Riverfront Elementary School," announced their teacher, Mrs. Hibbits.

A stunned silence followed. The children had been eager to spend a day at an inner-city school where they would have a chance to meet children of different races and backgrounds. They had not, however, been prepared for such a run-down school building.

Almost immediately after the bus stopped, the doors of the school opened and out filed a long line of children. Alex, Janie, and the others stared out the bus windows. The children from Riverfront Elementary all wore name tags on their clothing. Each held up a sign bearing the name of a visiting child seated on the bus. Alex scanned the signs, trying to spot her name. She hoped the name tag on her shirt was big enough for the right child from the other group to spot her.

"Come on, boys and girls," Mrs. Hibbits directed, "let's go meet some new friends."

Alex and Janie followed the others down the steps and out onto the pavement in front of the school. Almost immediately, two girls stepped up to them.

"Hi, I'm Cassandra Whitaker," said one of the girls to Alex. "I'll show you around while you're here."

"Great!" Alex replied, shaking Cassandra's hand gratefully. She liked Cassandra immediately. She was a tall, sturdy-looking African-American girl with a friendly smile.

Janie's friend was also African-American. Her name was Glenda. The four girls walked inside the school building together. Cassandra and Glenda led Alex and Janie down a wide hallway to a classroom. Alex sat down in a chair beside Cassandra's desk, while Janie sat beside Glenda.

As the day went by, Alex and Janie noticed several disturbing things about the school. That evening, Alex told her family all about her day at the inner-city school.

"The building was so cold, my toes froze!" Alex exclaimed. "They didn't have any computers, and hardly any balls at recess. But the thing that really got to me was the library," Alex said. "They hardly had any books, and the ones they did have were so old and dingy that nobody wants to even touch them."

"Oh, that's too bad," Mother replied. "It's so important for children to have good books to read."

"Yeah," Alex said. "Cassandra said that nobody ever checks out a library book."

After dinner, Alex went upstairs to her bedroom. She stared at the rows of books upon her bookshelves.

"There must be a way to help Cassandra's school get books for their library," Alex told herself. "I feel so sorry for them." Suddenly, Alex snapped her fingers. "I know! I'll ask the Lord about it. Maybe He'll tell me what to do."

Alex bowed her head. "Dear Lord Jesus," she prayed, "please tell me how I can help Cassandra's school get books for their library. I pray in Your name. Amen."

Then, as Alex continued to stare at

her bookshelf, an idea came into her mind. "Brussels sprouts!" Alex jumped up and raced down the curved stairway that led from her second-story bedroom to the front hallway. Alex found her parents in the family room.

"Guess what?" Alex asked her parents excitedly. "I prayed about Cassandra's library and I just got this terrific idea!" she exclaimed. "I'd like to give them my old books! Is that okay with you?"

"That's a wonderful idea," her parents agreed. "Why don't you ask your teacher about it?" they suggested.

The next day, Alex got to school early. She ran straight to her teacher's desk and told Mrs. Hibbits her idea.

Mrs. Hibbits exclaimed, "Alex, that's a wonderful idea! Maybe we could even get the whole school involved. I'll talk to the principal about it today." Mrs. Hibbits patted Alex's arm.

The call for books spread rapidly throughout the school. Everyone was enthusiastic about Alex's idea. Her class collected used books from students, friends, and neighbors. Soon boxes overflowing with children's books lined the back wall of the classroom.

$23 \times 14 =$

$16 \times 10 =$

"You wouldn't believe how many books we got already," Alex told her parents one evening at dinnertime. "The Lord sure answered my prayer in a big way. We started out with just my old books, but now we have more than two hundred!"

Mother and Father smiled. "That's what I call a mustard seed moment," said Mother.

"Huh?" Alex frowned. "What's a mustard seed?"

"It is one of the smallest of seeds, but when it's planted, it grows into a big tree," Mother replied. "Jesus said that if you have faith as big as a mustard seed, you can move mountains with it."

"Oh, I get it," replied Alex. "You mean that even if you start with something small, God can make it into something big."

"Exactly," said Mother.

The next day, Alex and her classmates again rode the bus to Riverfront Elementary School. Many large boxes filled with books were stacked at the back of the bus.

The bus pulled into the Riverfront school driveway. A crowd of children from the school met Alex and her classmates as they stepped from the bus. Cassandra ran up to Alex and hugged her.

As each box of books was pulled off the bus and carried into the school, the children from both schools cheered and shouted with joy. As Alex cheered and shouted with Cassandra and the others, she thought of what her mother had said the night before.

"You sure make good mustard seed moments, Lord!" Alex cried.

"What did you say?" Cassandra asked Alex, a puzzled look on her face.

"I'll tell you all about it inside," promised Alex. As she took Cassandra's arm and followed her inside the school, a flash of sunlight dazzled her eyes for an instant, then disappeared behind the clouds again.

He winked at me! God winked at me! Alex thought. She smiled broadly and then skipped happily into the school building with Cassandra.

Amen.

How did Alex want to help the children at the Riverfront school? How did God make the idea bigger and better? What did Mother mean about a mustard seed moment? Do you think God could give you a mustard seed moment? Why don't you ask Him?

In this story, the food from the Bible is:

God makes small things big.

Surprise
Performance

Go easy on others; then they will
do the same for you.
Luke 6:37b

ALEX listened as the group of boys
hurled cruel insults at another boy in
their class.

"Hey, Patsy, what's the matter? Are
you afraid of the ball?"

"Yeah, Patsy, maybe you oughta go
play on the swings with the kinder-
gartners!"

The small, blond-haired boy stumbled
away from the ball field. He did not look
back as he walked to the fence at the
back of the playground. He leaned

against the fence, his face turned away from the ball field and the jeering boys.

Alex frowned at a boy named Eddie. "You shouldn't be so hard on Patrick," she told him.

"Aw, he's just a wimp," Eddie replied. "Come on, Alex, just pitch another ball."

Still frowning, Alex started her windup. She was beginning to regret that she had agreed to pitch for Eddie's team. Alex threw a pitch. The batter swung and missed.

"Strike three!" cried the boy who was playing umpire. "That's three outs!"

"Way to go, Alex!" her team cried as they hurried off the field for their turn at bat.

"Hey, Alex, where ya going?" Eddie called after her as Alex trotted behind the backstop and away from the field.

"I'm gonna go talk to Patrick!" Alex hollered back at Eddie.

She slowed down as she neared the fence and the boy the others so cruelly called "Patsy."

"Uh, hi," Alex said as she came to stand beside Patrick. "You shouldn't let Eddie get to you. He's always being a jerk."

"They're all jerks," Patrick replied with a sniff. "They don't even try to understand why I can't play ball with them."

"Why don't you tell me?" Alex asked him. "I'll try to understand."

Patrick looked down at the ground. "Do you promise not to laugh?" he asked finally.

"Sure," Alex replied.

"Okay," Patrick replied. "I can't play ball because I'm going to play the leading part in the musical *Oliver* this summer at the Starlight Theatre. I had to promise the director of the show that I would not do anything that might injure me. So I can't play any sports until after the show is over."

"Brussels sprouts!" Alex whistled. "The Starlight Theatre is a neat place. We went there once to see *Peter Pan*.

How'd you get to be in one of their shows?"

"Oh, I've been acting and singing for a long time," Patrick replied. "My voice teacher recommended me for the part, so I tried out and got it."

"But didn't you tell Eddie and the other boys about it so they'd know why you can't play ball?" Alex asked Patrick.

"Yeah, I told them. They just laughed at me and called me Patsy," Patrick scowled.

"Oh, don't pay attention to them," Alex sighed. "They're just dopes. I think what you're doing is really neat!"

"Thanks," Patrick smiled.

Just then, the bell rang, signaling the end of afternoon recess. "You go inside ahead of me," Alex told Patrick. "I want to talk to Eddie."

Alex ran over to Eddie as he and the others were leaving the ball field. "Eddie, don't be so mean to Patrick," Alex said. "He can't play sports right now because he's going to be in a musical at the Starlight Theatre."

"I know, I know," Eddie snarled. "That's the dumbest thing I ever heard."

"It's not dumb! It's neat!" Alex retorted. "You're just jealous because you don't have his kind of talent."

"Me? Jealous of Patsy?" Eddie burst out laughing.

"Well, you oughta quit making fun of him," Alex insisted. "You're not supposed to judge people who are different than you!"

"Oh, be quiet, Miss Know-It-All," Eddie replied.

Back in the classroom, their teacher, Mrs. Hibbits, had an announcement. "Children," she said, "our school has decided to adopt a refugee family from Bosnia. We need to do something to raise money for them. We are thinking of having a bake sale along with some kind of special entertainment. If you have any suggestions for the entertainment, please let me know."

After school, Alex and Patrick talked

to Mrs. Hibbits. "We have an idea for special entertainment at your bake sale," Alex told the teacher excitedly.

"Oh?" Mrs. Hibbits looked from Alex to Patrick and back to Alex again. "What's that?" she asked.

"Patrick is going to be the star in *Oliver* this summer at the Starlight Theatre," Alex informed the teacher. "He and maybe some of the others from the musical could sing at the bake sale."

"Why, I think that's a wonderful idea!" Mrs. Hibbits exclaimed. "I'm sure it would be a big hit and would raise lots of money for our refugee family."

Arrangements were made for the bake sale to be held in two weeks. Patrick busily rehearsed his songs. On the night of the bake sale, Alex met Patrick on the school's stage an hour before the performance. Two other actors were with him. Alex had a special job. She was to stay backstage during the performance and help with costumes and props.

The school auditorium slowly filled up. Alex peeked out at the crowd from behind the stage curtain.

"Eddie and his friends are in the front row," she whispered to Patrick.

"Good," Patrick smiled. "That will give me a chance to really blast them!"

Soon the lights dimmed. Patrick and the other actors gave a splendid performance that was over much too quickly for Alex.

The audience rose to its feet and applauded Patrick and his friends loudly. Alex smiled when Eddie and his friends stumbled to their feet and joined in the applause.

Afterward, Eddie came over to where Alex and Patrick were munching on brownies, chocolate chip cookies, and peanut butter bars.

"Wow, where'd you learn to sing like that?" Eddie asked Patrick.

Patrick shrugged. "I dunno. I guess I've had good voice teachers."

"Well, uh, it was really good," Eddie said awkwardly. "Uh, I'm sorry for all the trouble I gave you. I can see now why you wouldn't want to take a chance on getting hurt and missing your show."

"Thanks," Patrick smiled at Eddie. "Maybe we can be friends now?" he asked.

"You can count on it," Eddie agreed.

Amen.

Food for Thought

Why did Eddie think Patrick was a wimp? How did Alex help discover Patrick's surprise talent? Many people have hidden talents that are waiting to be discovered. How about you?

In this story, the food from the Bible is:

Do not criticize others.

Rotten Revenge

Never pay back evil for evil.
Romans 12:17a

ALEX stood with the rest of the class and recited the Pledge of Allegiance. She tried to ignore the whispers and giggles all around her. Why did she have to sit in the middle of a group of boys? Alex sighed. They were acting even more terrible than usual today.

The Pledge of Allegiance ended, and everyone sat down. But when Alex sat down, she sat on something soft and squishy that had not been on her chair before.

BTHMMMMMMMPF! went a loud and disgusting noise.

Alex jumped up immediately. She turned bright red. The boys around her desk collapsed with laughter.

"What was that?" Mrs. Hibbits wanted to know.

Alex pulled a small, black cushion off her chair and handed it to her teacher. "Someone put this on my chair," Alex told her. She glared at the boys.

Mrs. Hibbits pressed on the center of the cushion. BTHMMMMMMMPF! The cushion repeated. This time, the whole class broke into laughter.

"Whose cushion is this?" Mrs. Hibbits asked. The teacher wore a no-nonsense look.

Eddie Thompson slowly raised his hand.

"I should have known," Mrs. Hibbits sighed. "I want you to take the cushion home tonight and do not bring it back again," Mrs. Hibbits sternly told Eddie. "You may spend your morning recess writing an apology to Alex."

Alex waited until the teacher had turned her back, then she stuck her tongue out at Eddie. She was very angry. Eddie was always causing her trouble. If he did one more thing to her today, she was going to let him have it!

The morning passed quickly. Recess came and went. When Eddie handed Alex his apology note, she tore it up and threw it away. Soon it was time for lunch.

"Alex, why don't you just forget about Eddie?" Janie asked. "He's already been punished for what he did."

"How can I forget it?" Alex retorted. "Eddie and his stupid friends are always doing something to me. I tell you, I've just about had it!"

Just then, Eddie and Joshua passed the girls' lunch table on their way out to recess. The boys leaned over and shouted in Alex's ear, "BTHMMMMMMMPF!"

Alex stood up quickly and swung at them, but missed. "I'm gonna get them if it's the last thing I do!" Alex cried.

"Alex, take it easy," Janie tried to calm her friend.

"Go on out to recess, Janie," Alex told her. "I'm gonna stay inside and figure out a way to get back at Eddie."

Alex sat at the lunch table and thought and thought. She did not notice that the rest of the children had left the cafeteria and she was the only one left.

"You have to go outside for recess with the other children," the teacher on cafeteria duty said to Alex.

Alex stood up and left the room. But instead of going outside with the others, she doubled back down the hall to her own classroom. No one was in the room. Alex sat down at her desk. Eddie Thompson had ruined her day! How was she going to get even?

Angrily, Alex began rummaging through her desk. Suddenly, underneath a pile of notebook paper, her hands clasped an unfamiliar object. Pulling it out, Alex saw that it was a tube of contact cement. She had brought it from home for a social studies poster project. Alex stared at the tube for a full two minutes. A sly smile began to cover her face.

"Of course!" Alex exclaimed and quickly went to work.

Alex glanced at the clock and noticed that there were only a few minutes left for recess. She hurried out of the room and down the hall. Waiting until the teacher on playground duty turned her back, Alex sneaked out onto the playground.

"Alex, where have you been?" Janie

wanted to know, as soon as Alex joined her friend on the jungle gym.

"I've been getting revenge, Janie," Alex replied. "Sweet revenge!"

"What do you mean?" Janie cried. "Alex, what have you done?"

"Just watch Eddie Thompson when he comes in from recess," Alex told her.

When the bell rang to end recess, Alex and Janie excitedly rushed to be the first ones into the classroom. They watched Eddie Thompson's every move. Of course, he was one of the last to come in and take his seat. Alex smirked as Eddie plopped down hard into his chair.

"Please take out your reading books," Mrs. Hibbits told the class.

Alex grinned as she watched Eddie struggle with the top of his desk.

"Hey, there's something wrong with my desk!" the bully cried. "It won't open." He tried to stand up to get a better grip on the desk top, but found he couldn't.

With a loud popping and tearing sound, Eddie broke free of his chair.

Strands of glue tore from the chair and stuck to the seat of Eddie's pants. He then pulled at the top of his desk, finally wrenching it open. Clumps of sticky cement hung down all around the top edges of the desk.

Alex had lined the edges of Eddie's desk with the cement and put a large glop of it on his seat.

"YUCK!" Eddie cried.

Everyone began to laugh, but no one more loudly than Alex. She laughed so hard, she fell from her chair. It took Mrs. Hibbits several minutes to restore order in the classroom.

"This is a serious offense against another person and against school property," Mrs. Hibbits sternly told the class. "I want to know who is responsible!"

Alex ducked her head at the sight of her teacher's angry gaze. Suddenly, revenge did not seem quite so sweet. She had been so busy trying to get back at Eddie, she had not thought about the consequences.

Slowly, very slowly, under the frightful stare of her teacher and in the heavy silence of the room, Alex raised her hand. She followed her teacher out into the hallway.

"Alex, what made you do such a terrible thing?" asked Mrs. Hibbits as soon as she closed the door to the classroom.

As Alex told her teacher about the mean things Eddie had done and how she had wanted to get even with him, she realized that her words sounded silly and childish. She hung her head. She realized that by her very act of revenge, she had become as guilty as Eddie Thompson.

"Do you see now, Alex, that revenge doesn't work?" her teacher asked quietly.

"Yeah, I see that now," Alex nodded her head slowly. "I did something just as bad as Eddie did. I wish I never would have tried to get even with him."

"Sometimes we have to learn the hard way," Mrs. Hibbits told Alex. She patted Alex's shoulder and then led her to the principal's office.

Amen.

 Food for Thought

Why did Alex want to get back at Eddie Thompson? What did Alex learn about getting revenge? In the Bible, Jesus told us not to seek revenge. Why is that good advice?

In this story, the food from the Bible is:

God doesn't want us to seek revenge.

Treasure Disasters

Lay up for yourselves treasures in heaven,
where neither moth nor rust destroys, and
where thieves do not break in or steal.
Matthew 6:20 (NASB)

DAD, how do you lay up treasure in heaven?" Alex asked her father one Sunday after church. "Our Sunday school teacher told us that Jesus said to lay up treasure in heaven, but I'm not sure I understand what that means."

"It means to do good things here on earth that will earn you a reward in heaven," Father answered. "God notices everything you do, and when you do good things, He saves treasure for you. Then when you get to heaven, you have all the treasure that you earned."

"That's neat!" Alex exclaimed. "I'm going to start earning treasure right away!"

The next morning, Alex was up bright and early. It was a beautiful summer day, and she did not want to miss any of it. Right after breakfast, Alex gathered up her softball mitt and a ball. She was about to head out the back door to practice her pitching, when she noticed her big, black dog, T-Bone, sitting patiently on the kitchen floor. T-Bone gripped his leash in his mouth and stared at Mother.

"T-Bone, I can't take you for a walk right now," Mother told the big dog. "I have to finish washing these dishes."

"I'll take T-Bone for a walk," Alex volunteered.

"Why, Alex, that would be wonderful," Mother replied. "Thank you."

"Oh, sure," Alex shrugged. "I'm trying to do good things and store up treasure in heaven." She snapped the leash onto the black labrador's collar, and she and the big dog stepped outside for a walk.

"I know what we'll do," Alex said to T-Bone. "I'll take you for a real good walk. We'll go up to the school playground, and you can run around and gets lots of exercise!"

The big labrador wagged his tail. He and Alex raced to the playground. Alex unsnapped T-Bone's leash, and she and the dog had a great time leaping and chasing each other about the playground.

Suddenly, however, another dog came on the scene. T-Bone trotted over to the other dog. They sniffed each other and then, without warning, both dogs took off running toward the creek that ran behind the school.

"T-Bone, come back here!" Alex cried, but the big labrador was having too much fun with his new friend to pay attention to Alex.

The two dogs ran down the muddy creek bank. Alex followed as fast as she could, slipping and sliding in the mud. Finally, she caught up with them when the dogs halted to sniff an old tin can.

"Brussels sprouts! T-Bone, you and I are going to be in trouble!" Alex told the dog as she looked at his mud-coated fur and her mud-splattered clothes.

"Alex! What in the world happened?" Mother frowned when the two of them returned home.

"I was just trying to give T-Bone extra exercise," Alex replied. She told Mother what had happened at the school playground and the creek

"Well, now I'll give you both some extra exercise," Mother said, dragging out a big, round washtub and setting it up on the patio. "You may give T-Bone a bath," Mother said as she handed Alex a towel and a bottle of dog shampoo.

Alex had just worked up a good lather on T-Bone when sudden, frantic shouts reached her ears.

"Help! Help!"

Alex stood and looked across her

backyard into Jason's backyard. What she saw made her laugh. Her little brother, Rudy, was suspended in midair, hanging from a limb in Jason's tree.

"Help!" Rudy called to her again. "I can't get down!"

Leaving T-Bone to soak in the tub, Alex jumped the fence between the yards and hurried to stand right beneath Rudy.

Gazing up at her brother, Alex chuckled, "Rudy, I think you have a problem."

"Alex, it's not funny! Get me down!" Rudy cried.

"Okay, hold on. You're up way too high for me to reach. I gotta get something to stand on," Alex told him.

Rushing back to her own house, Alex ran to the garage and yanked one of Father's ladders off its hook. She tried to hoist it over her head as she had seen Father do many times. The weight of the ladder, however, was too much for Alex to handle. She and the ladder crashed backward, knocking over a stack of Mother's flowerpots, and sending Father's tools to the floor.

SLAM! BLAM! SHATTER!

"Alex! What are you doing?" Mother cried, opening the door that led from the kitchen to the garage. She stared in disbelief at the broken flowerpots, the tools, the ladder, and Alex, all lying together on the garage floor.

"Uh, sorry, Mom," Alex struggled to her feet. "I was getting the ladder to rescue Rudy out of Jason's tree."

"What?" Mother asked. She hurried out of the garage and gazed into Jason's backyard. "Oh, my goodness!" Mother cried when she saw Rudy dangling high from the tree limb.

Mother and Alex quickly carried the ladder into Jason's backyard. Then Mother climbed the ladder and rescued Rudy.

"What were you doing up there?" Mother asked her son, as soon as he was safely back on the ground.

"I was trying to get my kite," Rudy explained as he rubbed his stiff and sore arms. "It's stuck up there." He pointed to the top of the tree.

"We'll get it down later," Mother told him. Alex, Rudy, and Mother walked to their own backyard. When they reached the patio, however, a disastrous sight met their eyes.

While Alex was rescuing Rudy, T-Bone had flipped the washtub upside down. It had landed on top of a flower box full of Mother's prized geraniums. Sudsy water covered the patio. T-Bone, soaking wet from head to toe and looking quite pleased with himself, was resting on Mother's favorite lounge chair.

"Oh, no!" Alex cried in dismay.

"Looks like you get a chance to earn more treasure by cleaning the patio, the garage, and the dog," Mother told Alex.

That evening after dinner, Alex climbed onto Father's lap as he sat in his big chair. "You know, trying to lay up heavenly treasure can be a lot harder than you think," she told him. Father laughed as Alex told him all about her day.

"Sounds like you've had a rough one," Father said when she was finished, "but don't give up! I'm sure God understands. He might even give you extra treasure because you tried so hard."

"Do you really think so?" Alex asked hopefully.

"I think you can count on it," Father replied.

Alex hugged her father. Then she said, "Dad, does God ever give us treasure here on earth?"

Father put his arms around Alex and held her tight. "He sure does, Firecracker. You are my treasure," he whispered. "You are my treasure from God."

Amen.

 ## Food for Thought

What are some of the ways Alex tried to store treasure in heaven? What are some ways you could store up heavenly treasure? God has given us many ways to store up treasure in heaven. Start adding to your treasure chest today!

In this story, the food from the Bible is:

Store up heavenly treasure.

The Secret Password

Yes, be bold and strong! Banish fear and doubt! For remember, the Lord your God is with you wherever you go.
Joshua 1:9

WELL, you're finally here," Amanda said as she came to the back gate. "By the time all your mothers called my mother, I thought we'd never get to swim!"

Amanda was Alex's neighbor. They had a new swimming pool, and she had invited Alex and her friends to come over to swim.

"Sorry," Alex and Janie said, thoroughly embarrassed.

"Well, you can all still be members of my secret club," Amanda informed them. "Only members can swim in my pool. That way, we won't get anybody in here that we don't want."

"Cool," Janie and Julie replied. They liked the idea of a swimming club. Lorraine smiled shyly and did not say anything. Only Alex frowned at the idea.

"What kind of a club is it?" Alex asked, becoming a little suspicious. She knew Amanda well enough to know that she had a mean streak and could be cruel.

"Oh, it's just a club where we get together and swim and have picnics and stuff," Amanda answered Alex, sounding a bit annoyed. "You know, summer fun in the sun!"

"Great!" the others shouted.

"Do we have to do anything to be in the club?" Alex wanted to know. She felt something had to be wrong with the idea. She just didn't know what it was.

"No," Amanda answered. "You just have to say the secret password."

"What is the secret password?" Alex asked, getting more and more irritated with Amanda's bossy attitude.

Amanda grinned at Alex. She waited until she had everyone's attention and then said, "The secret password is @#!*$#@$!@#!@$*#*$@#*!"

Everyone gasped in shock. Amanda had just rattled off a stream of the dirtiest words they had ever heard.

The children looked at one another with worried expressions. Amanda still wore a grin on her face. It was obvious that she enjoyed their discomfort.

"Aw, come on. It's a great password," Amanda finally broke the silence. "Let's all practice it out loud so we can get it right. Remember, if you can't say the password, you can't get inside the gate."

Amanda held up her hands as if getting ready to direct a choir. "Now repeat after me," she instructed, and again rattled off the string of nasty words. She waited for the others to repeat the words. No one made a sound. Everyone looked embarrassed.

"Come on, it's not hard," Amanda

insisted. But before she could repeat the dirty words again, Alex held up her hands.

"Stop!" Alex shouted at Amanda. "That is enough! This is wrong and you all know it," Alex told her friends. "Nobody should say those words. We should all leave!"

Alex turned and marched across the backyard to her own yard. None of her friends had followed her. They had not wanted to leave the big swimming pool with its slide and diving board.

Alex trudged inside her house. *I guess they said the password,* she thought gloomily. She shook her head

and stared out her second-story window. From it, Alex could see part of Amanda's yard and pool. She sighed wistfully as she watched her friends jump off the diving board and splash into the pool.

"Why aren't you swimming at Amanda's with your friends?" a voice asked quietly behind her. Alex turned to see Mother standing in the doorway.

Alex looked at Mother sadly. "Because I wouldn't say the password," she explained.

"The password?" Mother looked puzzled.

Alex told her mother all about Amanda's secret club and the nasty password she wanted the children to say.

"There was no way I was going to say those words," Alex told Mother.

"Good for you!" Mother responded. "I'm proud of you. It took a lot of courage for you to stand up to Amanda."

"Yeah, but I think I lost my friends by doing so," Alex sniffed.

"No, I don't think so," Mother patted her shoulder. "Just hang in there. In a while, your friends will realize that you were right."

Later that afternoon, Alex, Rudy, and Jason were in Alex's backyard practicing softball. Alex had not paid attention to the chattering girls as they swam and played noisily. Alex and the boys stopped their play, however, and looked up worriedly when a loud scream pierced the air. The gate to Amanda's yard flung open and out rushed Lorraine.

"ALEX!" screamed Lorraine, "HELP! THERE'S BEEN AN ACCIDENT!"

"Go get Mom!" Alex told Rudy. She leaped over her backyard fence and ran to Amanda's yard. Following Lorraine through the gate, Alex gasped to see Janie struggling to swim to the side of the pool. Janie was crying. Her right hand was raised to her ear. Red blood oozed onto Janie's fingers.

"She's all right," Amanda scowled. "It's only a little cut. What a crybaby!" Amanda jeered from the side of the pool. A second later, however, she changed her tune as Mother charged through the gate.

"Here, let me help you," Amanda said, suddenly trying to help Janie.

"Don't touch me!" Janie screamed at Amanda.

Mother helped Janie out of the water and looked at her ear. "It's going to be all right," she soothed Janie.

Wrapping a towel around Janie, Mother led her out the gate. Alex and the other girls followed. The last Alex saw of Amanda, she stood all alone in her swimming pool, an angry scowl covering her face.

"I'm never going back there again!" Janie cried. "You were right, Alex," she turned to her friend. "I should have listened to you."

"Yeah," Alex's other friends agreed. "Amanda was terrible. She told Janie she had to do a back dive off the board or she couldn't stay in the club!"

"That's how I hurt my ear," Janie sniffed. "I hit my head on the diving board."

"We're never going back to Amanda's again," the girls promised Alex. "We're sorry we didn't listen to you in the first place."

"Oh, that's all right," Alex replied. She smiled at her mother. She had done the right thing. It had been hard, but she had found the courage to stand up for what she knew was right.

Amen.

 ## Food for Thought

Why did Alex leave Amanda's pool? Why didn't her friends leave with her? How did Alex show courage? Where did she get her courage and strength?

In this story, the food from the Bible is:

Be courageous for what's right.

A New Sister

For God sometimes uses sorrow in our
lives to help us turn away from sin
and seek eternal life.
II Corinthians 7:10a

BUT why did Grandpa Jim have to die?"
Rudy asked his parents from the
backseat of the family station wagon.

Mother turned around and looked
back at Rudy. "Everybody has to die
sometime, Rudy," she said. "Grandpa
Jim was old and sick. It must have been
the right time for him to die. Only God
knows the right time for each person."

Alex sat next to Rudy in the backseat.
"Was Grandpa Jim a Christian?" Alex
asked Mother.

"Yes," Mother answered.

"Then he's in heaven right now," Alex said confidently. "Grandpa Jim will get to live with Jesus and the angels."

"And he won't ever be sick again," added Rudy.

"Then why is everyone so sad?" Barbara asked. "We ought to be happy for Grandpa Jim. He's finally reached his heavenly home."

"You're right, Barbara," Mother agreed. "We ought to be happy for Grandpa Jim. He lived a long life, and now he's gone home. Everyone is so sad because we will miss him."

"But we'll see him again when we get to heaven," Alex said.

"You're right," Mother agreed, "and won't that be a happy time? We'll all be home for good, and we won't ever be sad or worried again."

"Yeah, because everything is perfect in heaven," added Alex. "I just hope God builds lots of softball fields for me!"

Everybody laughed.

"What do you think, Dad?" Barbara asked her father. "Do you think there will be softball fields in heaven?"

"Well," Father rubbed his chin, "I think heaven will be perfect for each person there," he answered. "So, if Alex wants softball fields, I wouldn't be surprised if the Lord gives her softball fields."

"Well, then I better keep practicing my pitching," Alex said. "I wanna be really good when I pitch in heaven!"

Again, they all laughed.

After driving several more hours, the family finally pulled up in front of a big, white house. It was Grandpa Jim and Grandma Rose's house. Now Grandma Rose would live there by herself.

"Hi, Alex!" called a voice as soon as Alex stepped out of the car.

"Hi, Marjorie," Alex greeted her cousin. Marjorie and her family lived in a house just a block away from Grandma Rose.

Alex's aunt, uncle, and grandmother hurried out of the house to greet Alex and her family. Mother and Father hugged Grandma Rose. The elderly lady had tears in her eyes.

"I guess Grandma Rose will miss Grandpa Jim the most," Alex said to herself. When it was her turn, Alex hugged her grandmother tightly. She wished she could do something special for the elderly lady, but as she looked into her grandmother's eyes, she knew it was enough that she had come. It was enough that the family was there.

After the suitcases had all been carried inside and up to their rooms, Alex ran down to the kitchen. Her grandmother poured her a root beer. Grandma Rose always made sure to have Alex's favorite soft drink on hand. The drink always seemed to taste better out of one of Grandma Rose's light blue glasses with the tiny daisies painted around the rim.

Finally, after the rest of the family had settled in and were talking in the living room, Alex managed to sneak off with Marjorie. The two girls walked a little ways from the house and sat down under a large tree in the backyard.

"Is something the matter, Marjorie?" Alex asked. Her cousin had been unusually silent.

Marjorie sighed. "I guess I'm really sad about Grandpa Jim. He was my

special friend, and now he's gone and I'll never see him again!"

"Oh, yes, you will," Alex tried to cheer her cousin. "You'll see him in heaven."

"How do you know he's in heaven?" Marjorie asked.

"Because he was a Christian," Alex told her. "All Christians go to heaven."

"Are you a Christian?" Marjorie asked Alex.

"Yes," Alex said simply.

"What does it mean to be a Christian?"

"Well," Alex spoke slowly and carefully, "a Christian believes that Jesus is the Son of God, and that He came to earth and died for our sins. We believe that Jesus was crucified and rose from the dead and went to heaven. When we die, we will also go to heaven to live with Him forever."

"So, because Grandpa Jim was a Christian, he is living with Jesus right now?" Marjorie asked.

"Yeah," Alex replied. She hesitated a moment and then asked, "Marjorie, are you a Christian?"

"I guess not," Marjorie said sadly. "My family doesn't even go to church."

"But you can still be a Christian anyway," Alex told her. "All you have to do is believe in Jesus and ask Him to come into your heart."

"Really?" Marjorie looked hopeful.

"That's all I have to do?"

"Yes," replied Alex. "Why don't you do it right now?"

"Okay, tell me what to say," said Marjorie.

"Just tell Him you believe in Him and you want to be a Christian. Ask Him to forgive your sins and come into your heart," Alex instructed.

"Okay." Marjorie got on her knees and bowed her head. "Dear Jesus," she prayed, "I believe in You, and I want to be a Christian like Alex. Please forgive me for my sins and please come into my heart. Amen."

"Amen," Alex repeated. She looked at her cousin. Instead of grief, there was a special joy in Marjorie's eyes. Alex felt the joy too. It was wonderful that where there had been such sadness before, now there was great happiness.

Alex squeezed Marjorie's hand as they walked back to the house. "Now we are sisters and part of God's family," Alex whispered to her cousin. She looked up at the sky. She was certain Grandpa Jim was watching them right now. How happy he must be, she thought, to know that Marjorie had just become a Christian.

"Thank You, Lord Jesus," Alex prayed silently. "Thank You for my new sister, Marjorie."

Amen.

 Food for Thought

Why was Marjorie so sad? How did Alex help her find happiness in the middle of such a sad time? Sometimes, it takes a tragedy to turn people to Jesus. Why do you think that is true?

In this story, the food from the Bible is:

Sorrow can turn people to God.

Trouble for Janie

A life of doing right is the wisest life there is.
Proverbs 4:11b

"ALEX! Psst, Alex!" whispered a voice directly behind her.

Alex tried to ignore the whisper. It had come from Joshua Barton, one of the chief troublemakers in her class. Unfortunately, he sat at a desk directly behind her.

"Alex!" Joshua tried again. This time, a finger jabbed the middle of her back.

Alex turned halfway around in her chair and growled, "What do you want?"

"What's the answer to question four?" Joshua hissed.

"I'm not telling you!" Alex exclaimed. She turned back around to sit straight in her chair. That did it! That was all she could take of Joshua Barton. Yesterday, he knocked her books to the floor. This morning, he hooked paper clips in her hair. Now, he wanted her to give him the answers to the math test. He wanted her to cheat!

"Come on, Alex, just tell me the answer to question four," Joshua continued to whisper.

"I do not cheat," Alex informed Joshua. She bent over her test paper, shielding her answers with her left hand.

"Okay, Miss Goody-goody," Joshua snarled. He leaned across the aisle to the next row of desks.

"Hey, Janie," Joshua whispered. "What's the answer to number four?"

To Alex's dismay, Janie gave Joshua the answer immediately.

"Brussels sprouts, Janie, that's cheating!" Alex whispered to her best friend.

"Oh, Alex," Janie shrugged, "don't worry about it."

Red-faced, Alex stared back down at her paper. For the rest of the period, she did her best to ignore Janie and Joshua as they compared answers to all the test questions. Alex wished they sat at the front of the classroom instead of the very back, and that their teacher, Mrs. Hibbits, would hear them and make them stop.

Finally, Mrs. Hibbits called an end to the test and collected the papers. She told the class to line up at the door to go to the lunchroom. Joshua Barton wore a smug expression on his face when he ran to join his friends in line. Alex did not speak to Janie, even though her best friend walked next to her in line. She waited until they got their lunch trays and sat down at one of the long tables in the cafeteria.

"I can't believe you gave Joshua all the answers to the math test," Alex frowned at Janie.

"Oh, Alex, it was just one little test," Janie replied. "It doesn't matter that much."

"Doesn't matter?" Alex exclaimed. "It's cheating!"

"Oh, it's not cheating very much," Janie said, calmly biting into a piece of pizza. "Besides, I think Joshua Barton is really cute, especially the way he screws up his eyes and kinda squints when he talks to you," Janie giggled, and so did the other girls at the table.

"Janie!" Alex almost shouted in frustration. "You mean you cheated for someone just because he's cute and squints his eyes at you?"

This time the girls at the table laughed so loud the teacher on duty had to tell them to be quiet.

"Oh, Alex," Janie said as soon as the teacher left, "you are such an old fuddy-duddy!"

"Well, I may be an old fuddy-duddy, but at least I'm an honest one," Alex retorted. "I don't believe in doing wrong things just because someone asks me to. I believe in doing right and standing up for what I believe!"

With that, Alex left the lunch table, not even bothering to finish her meal. Standing beside the cafeteria's double doors, Alex waited for the bell that signaled recess. When it rang, she hurried outside to the playground.

Alex ran toward the big swing set that sat at the back of the playground. Her friends Julie and Lorraine ran after her. The three girls jumped on swings. Alex felt better as she pumped her legs, making the swing go higher and higher.

Out of the corner of her eye, she watched Janie and a group of girls clustered around the teeter-totters. They talked and laughed loudly. Alex was sure they were laughing at her.

It wasn't long, however, before Alex saw her teacher, Mrs. Hibbits, march out of the building and down the steps to the playground. Mrs. Hibbits made a straight line toward Janie and her friends.

Even from the swing set, Alex could see that Mrs. Hibbits did not look happy. She watched as the teacher motioned for Janie to go with her. Mrs. Hibbits then called to Joshua Barton. Alex and her friends gasped as Janie and Joshua followed Mrs. Hibbits back inside the school building.

"Do you think they got caught cheating?" Julie asked Alex as the girls dragged their feet on the ground to slow their swings.

"I dunno," Alex replied. "It kind of looks that way."

For the rest of the recess, the girls talked about and wondered what was happening to Janie and Joshua. They did not find out when they went inside after recess. Janie and Joshua were not at their desks. Mrs. Hibbits continued to teach the class as if nothing had happened.

Later in the day, Janie and Joshua returned. Alex noticed Janie's red, swollen eyes and tearstained face as she walked quickly to her desk and took her seat. Joshua did not look much better. Neither of them spoke a word for the rest of the afternoon.

Alex did not find out what happened to Janie until after school. As they walked home, Janie told her how she and Joshua were taken to the principal's office and severely reprimanded for cheating on the math test.

"But how'd Mrs. Hibbits know you cheated?" Alex asked, puzzled. "She didn't say anything about it while you were taking the test."

"Mrs. Hibbits said she had suspected

that we were cheating, but it wasn't until she saw that all of our answers were exactly the same that she knew for sure," Janie explained.

"I'm sorry for you, Janie," Alex patted her friend's shoulder.

"Oh, it was my own stupid fault!" Janie sighed. "You were right, Alex. Cheating on the test was wrong. I've been thinking a lot about it, and I'm going to do things the right way, just like you said. I'm going to stand up for what I believe and not get talked into doing things I know are wrong!"

"Good for you," Alex hugged her best friend and then winked. "Does that go for cute boys, too? If they ask you to do something wrong, will you tell them to forget it?"

"You better believe I will!" Janie shouted. She and Alex laughed and laughed.

Amen.

Food for Thought

Is it ever okay to cheat, even just a little bit? How did Alex stand up for what she believed? Who do you think made the right decision—Alex or Janie?

In this story, the food from the Bible is:

Do what is right.

Birthday Blues

Work hard and cheerfully at all you do, just as
though you were working for the Lord.
Colossians 3:23a

ALEX, I think you and Julie should
make the plans and fill out the
invitations for Janie's birthday party
before you watch your movies," said
Mother.

"But, Mom, we rented two special
movies, and we won't have time to watch
them if we don't start now," Alex told
her mother.

"Yes, you will," Mother glanced at the
kitchen clock. "It's still early."

"But we gotta have time to make

popcorn and chocolate milk shakes," added Alex.

"Alex," Mother said in a way that meant no more arguing, "Julie is spending the night so that you can both plan a birthday party for Janie."

"Okay," Alex put away the ice cream and chocolate syrup. She and Julie trudged back upstairs to Alex's bedroom.

"Let's get the invitations done real fast," Alex told Julie, pulling a packet of eight invitations off her desk. She handed Julie a pen and got one for herself.

"How do we fill out the invitations?" Julie asked.

"Just write that the party is for Janie's birthday, and write down my address and the date of the party," Alex told her. "Oh, yeah, we better put down that it's a surprise so nobody will tell Janie about it."

"Okay," Julie said. "What is the date of the party?" she asked a moment later.

"Let's see," Alex glanced at the calendar on her wall. "The party is next

Friday, and that will be April 19."

The two girls scribbled out the invitations as fast as they could write. They stuffed them into the envelopes and wrote their friends' names on the outside of the envelopes.

"We'll pass these out at school on Monday," Alex told Julie. "Let's go show my mom that we got them all done. Then she'll let us watch the movies."

"But shouldn't we plan what we're gonna do at the party?" Julie asked.

Alex shrugged her shoulders. "Oh, we're just gonna play games and stuff, right?"

"And eat cake and ice cream," Julie reminded her.

"So it's no big deal," said Alex. "We can figure out the games later. We've got a whole week."

"Okay," Julie agreed. "Let's go watch the movies."

The two girls skipped down the stairs. Alex handed Mother the stack of invitations. "See, they're all done," she told Mother.

"Good," Mother looked at the envelopes. "Alex, these envelopes are sealed."

"Yeah," Alex nodded. "We got them all ready to pass out on Monday."

"But I wanted to check them," Mother frowned.

"Mom, I know how to fill out invitations," Alex replied as she rolled her eyes to the ceiling.

"Well, okay," Mother still stared at the envelopes in her hand.

"We're going to go watch our movies now," Alex told Mother. She pushed

Julie out of the kitchen toward the family room.

"Okay," Mother replied.

On Monday, Alex and Julie secretly passed out the invitations to their friends. On Tuesday, they decided which games they would play. On Wednesday they planned the decorations, and by Thursday, they had everything ready.

When Alex got home from school Friday afternoon, her older sister, Barbara, helped her hang pink streamers and balloons throughout the basement recreation room. The family ate an early dinner, and Julie came over at six thirty. She and Alex put their wrapped presents downstairs. Everything was ready. The girls sat in the living room to await their guests.

Alex looked at her watch. She frowned and tapped her foot. She was starting to get worried.

"Alex, it's after seven o'clock," Mother announced, stepping into the living room.

"I know, I know!" Alex cried. "I don't understand why no one is here. I told them six forty-five!"

"Why don't you call them and see what's happened?" Mother suggested.

"Okay," Alex ran into the kitchen. She dialed Lorraine's number.

"Hello," Lorraine answered.

"Lorraine! Where are you?" Alex shouted into the phone.

"Alex, is that you?" Lorraine sounded puzzled. "What do you mean? I'm right here at my house. You called me, remember?"

"Yeah, but why aren't you at my house?" Alex demanded. "Janie will be here any minute for her birthday party and it's supposed to be a surprise party!"

"What are you talking about, Alex?" Lorraine asked. "Tonight isn't Janie's birthday party. It's next Friday night, at least that's what your invitation said."

"What?" Alex almost screamed.

"Yeah," insisted Lorraine. "I have the invitation right here. It says April 19 on it. That's next week! Today is the twelfth."

"Oh, no," Alex dropped the telephone and sank to the floor in a heap.

"Alex, what's wrong?" Mother picked up the telephone. She listened quietly as Lorraine explained the situation to her.

"Thank you, Lorraine," Mother said and hung up the phone. She stared at Alex for a full minute. Finally, she said, "Do you know that if you hadn't been in such a hurry the other night, this would not have happened?"

"I know," Alex groaned. "Janie's party is ruined."

"That is your responsibility, Alex," Mother told her. "You need to learn to take the time to do things right. You should try to do your best in all that you do, even planning a friend's birthday party."

At that moment, the doorbell rang. Alex looked up at the clock. It was seven fifteen.

"That's Janie!" Alex cried in alarm. "What do I do?"

"You will have to go out there and explain to your friend why there are no guests at her birthday party," Mother replied.

Alex picked herself up off the floor and trudged to the door. Mother was right, of course. She had tried to take a shortcut in planning Janie's party, and now her best friend had to pay for it. It was a hard lesson to learn, but one Alex would never forget. From then on, she decided to always try to do her best.

Alex slowly opened the front door.

"Hi, Alex!" Janie said brightly.

"Uh, hi, Janie," Alex replied. "There's something I gotta tell you. . . . "

Amen.

Food for Thought

Why were Alex and Julie in such a hurry to fill out Janie's party invitations? What mistake did they make on the invitations? How did that ruin the party? Why is it important to try and do your best in everything that you do?

In this story, the food from the Bible is:

_____

Do your best at everything.

A Terrible
Rotten Day

We know how much God loves us because
we have felt his love and because we believe
him when he tells us that he loves us dearly.
I John 4:16a

ALEX, we gotta hurry! We're going to
be late for school!" Janie exclaimed as
she and Alex bustled down the Juniper
Street hill to Kingswood Elementary
School.

"I'm sorry, Janie, I can't help being
late!" Alex began to explain to her best
friend. "Everything bad happened to me
this morning. You won't believe it!
Barbara wouldn't let me in the
bathroom. She has some kind of fancy
art show after school and had to curl her

hair just right. Then I couldn't find my shoes, until I remembered I'd left 'em in the tree house yesterday. So, I had to climb up and get them. But while I was up in the tree, T-Bone ate my breakfast! The dumb dog got up on my chair and ate my scrambled eggs. The funny thing is that my dad was sitting there reading his newspaper and didn't even know it was T-Bone at the table instead of me!"

"Oh, Alex!" Janie cried, laughter tears running down her cheeks. "All of that didn't really happen, did it?"

"Yes, it did! Honest!"

"Uh-oh," Janie suddenly groaned. "Look down the hill! The safety patrols are going inside!"

Alex glanced ahead. "Come on, Janie!" she cried. "We're really late!"

The two girls ran at top speed down the rest of the hill to the busy intersection in front of the school. As soon as the light turned green, they rushed across the street. They ran up the walk, flung open the front door of the school building, and sprinted through the halls.

Turning a corner, they reached their classroom door the same moment their teacher, Mrs. Hibbits, stepped into the hallway to close the door.

"YAHHHHHH!" the teacher cried as the two girls knocked her against the wall, then tumbled over her. Alex and Janie slid headfirst into the classroom.

"RRRIIINNNGGG!" the school bell announced the beginning of class.

Mrs. Hibbits struggled to her feet. She stared at Alex and Janie with a frown on her face. "That was hardly the proper way to enter a classroom. You may both go to the principal's office and pick up a tardy slip."

Alex sighed. Her day was not improving.

"I'm sorry, Janie," she told her best friend as they trudged down the hall to the school office.

At lunchtime, their friends congratulated Alex and Janie on their entry into the classroom that morning. "That was hilarious!" laughed Julie and Lorraine.

"Oh, yeah, well, Mrs. Hibbits didn't think so," Alex said around bites of her hamburger. She was starving!

Suddenly, a wet glob of yellow goop hit Alex on the shoulder and oozed down her shirt.

"Mustard!" Janie exclaimed, staring at Alex's shirt.

Instantly, a group of boys sitting at another table broke into laughter.

"What's the matter, Alex? Don't you like mustard?" teased a boy named Nathan. He took a small yellow plastic packet from his tray and held it in his hands between both thumbs. Aiming the packet toward the girls, he pressed down hard with his thumbs. SQUIRT! Mustard flew out of the packet, spraying Alex again.

"YOU NERD!" Alex screamed at Nathan. "LOOK AT WHAT YOU'VE DONE TO MY SHIRT!" She ran and leaped on Nathan, pinning him to the floor and pounding him with her fists.

Soon, strong arms lifted Alex off Nathan. "We're going to the principal's office," a teacher said. Alex groaned. It would be her second trip to the office that day.

When Mother picked up Alex and her brother, Rudy, after school, she said, "Alex, when the principal called me, I couldn't believe it! Did you really jump on a boy in the cafeteria and punch him?"

"Yes, he squirted mustard all over me," Alex replied.

Mother frowned as she inspected the stains on Alex's clothes. "Well, you'll just have go to Barbara's art fair looking like that. There's no time to change."

Alex slumped against the car seat. The day had been so bad. She felt tired and dirty. She did not want to go to her sister's dopey art fair and look at dopey paintings.

"Well, how's my girl?" Father asked Alex when they met him at the high school.

"Don't ask," Alex growled. She grudgingly followed her parents and Rudy around the display of pictures painted by high school students. One of them caught her eye. It was a painting of Jesus sitting on a rock, holding children in His arms. After the kind of day Alex had experienced, she wished she could crawl into His lap too.

"Alex, here's a perfect picture for your room!" Mother suddenly exclaimed. It was another painting full of sports items, including softballs and soccer balls.

"Yeah," Alex mumbled, hardly looking at the painting.

"I think Alex and I will take a seat over there," Father told Mother, pointing to a row of chairs. "Come join us when you have finished looking at the paintings."

"What's the matter, Firecracker?" Father asked as soon as they sat down.

"Everything," Alex replied glumly. She began telling Father all about her rotten day. "I feel like I've done everything wrong today," she finished with a sigh.

"Come sit on my lap," Father lifted Alex in his arms. Alex leaned her head on Father's shoulder. She was suddenly reminded of the picture of Jesus holding the children in His lap. She told Father about it.

"I noticed that painting too," Father smiled. "Do you suppose those children needed extra comforting like you?"

"Maybe," Alex shrugged, "but God wouldn't want to hold me in His arms today—not after I've messed up so much."

"Of course He would," Father replied. "All of His children mess up, but that doesn't mean He doesn't love them. If human fathers can love their children even when they mess up, don't you think your heavenly Father can do the same?"

"Yeah, I guess so," Alex nodded.

Father and Alex were startled by Barbara suddenly appearing before them. "Alex! Guess what?" Barbara cried. "We just had a drawing for the artists and their families. I entered all of our names in it, and your name was drawn as the grand prize winner! You can take home any one of the paintings on display!"

Alex looked at Father in astonishment. Mother ran over to Alex excitedly. "I know which one you'll pick," she said. "The one with the softballs and soccer balls, right?"

Alex smiled at Father. She led her family back through the display of paintings, stopping at the one with Jesus holding the children on His lap.

"That is the one I want," Alex told her mother.

Father laughed his big booming laugh, and for the first time that day, Alex felt happy.

"Thanks, Lord," she whispered. "Thanks for showing me Your love."

Amen.

 Food for Thought

Do you ever have bad days like Alex? Do you feel as if nobody loves you? If you ever do, remember that your heavenly Father always loves you. He loves you whether you are big or small, bad or good, no matter what you look like or what you accomplish. He loves you with all of His love. You don't get just "a share" of His love. You get all of His love.

In this story, the food from the Bible is:

God loves you always.